DON'T KNOCK THE HUSTLE

STACY NELSON

GRIP PUBLISHING

DON'T KNOCK THE HUSTLE

GRIP PUBLISHING
PO BOX 742164
DALLAS TX 75374
469.740.7072

First printing November 2004
10 9 8 7 6 5 4 3 2 1
ISBN: 0-978-0-9761417-1-6
Revised publication July 2016
Library of Congress Control Number: 2004112485

Cover concept: Stacy Nelson
Cover design/typeset/graphics: Saeed Tahir

DEDICATIONS

I dedicate all of my works to the portal and vessel that brought me into existence...

MY DADDY and MY MOMMY

Things That Make You Wonder "What The Hell"

During December in Milwaukee, the fierce cold winds that blew thru the streets reaching up to fifteen miles per hour could make the tops of insecurely closed garbage cans rattle.

The few people on the streets walked briskly as if there were snakes at their feet all in an effort to offer the least possible exposed skin surface to the harsh winds. Wintertime in Milwaukee is usually so frosty and chilly that folks who knew that they had to be out in the weather, would need to sport two to three layers of clothing to stay insulated from the harsh, heartless cold.

In contrast, the summers in Milwaukee could get so passionately heated that folks who weren't fortunate to have a cooling system of some sort in their homes by way of an air conditioner that sat in a window or by way of central air, could possibly die of heat exhaustion.

Hot or cold, freezing or melting, the streets are mean, brutal, unfair and impartial no matter what the temperature decides to be. On the social tip, it really all just depended on who was on the streets, when they were on the bricks, where their particular location was and what the hell they were participating in or dodging at the time.

As on any street in America, all kind of folks can be witnessed strolling the blocks on a mission of some sort. Ever since the late seventies more and more were on missions to get high. Some folks were on the streets getting pimped whether they were man, woman or child. Some would be in the nearest alleyway or on apartment stoops trying to catch money gambling shooting craps. Stealing anything that could be taken and sold to make a profit of some sort was some folk's choice of living. Many even tried to do just enough to avoid going to jail or escape having to go back in on some far out shit.

In true life everyone has choices on how they want or care to live but some are forced into living a certain lifestyle.

From a true to life perspective, anyone is capable of being straight up criminally intentioned. Without the experience of having and utilizing street smarts there runs the risk of being legally blinded.

Appearances can be quite deceiving. For example, just because a man dons a nice suit does not mean that he is one hundred percent clean and void of committing any kind of crime. Nowadays, the major drug dealers and users dress impeccably, run major offices and work in the public eye. On the flip, just because a person sports worn out or baggy clothing doesn't necessarily mean that that individual is a bum, addict or a hustler of some sort.

Society has fucked up labels on people from the ghetto. Rural America tends to think that the ghetto only exists in poverty stricken areas. Many would argue that the word ghetto is a matter of the state of mind. Others would counter that the word ghetto refers to where you're at.

Stars are conceived and born in the ghetto, raised in the ghetto, live in the ghetto and kick it in the ghetto.

Anyhow, watching the people on the chilly streets made me thankful to have found a hooptie with working heat to last me throughout the winter. There's nothing worse than having to make way in a ride without heat on a cold ass day with no defrost to keep the windows clear or to provide a little bit of warmth.

Shit, I rode in cars like that before, hell who hasn't? It was no joking matter when it came to the point of my cloud of breath standing suspended in midair instead of evaporating. A brother's hands got all wrinkled and shriveled from the bite of the cold air and being that I'm too damn cool for gloves when I finally did make it inside a warmer climate, I damn near screamed like a bitch in a horror flick trying to defrost.

On my way to see my guy Loc, I peeped a few of his customers meandering up and down the block aimlessly as if they had somewhere important to be. In fact they did have to be somewhere important …wherever the crack was located.

Baseheads seemed to take over the neighborhood more and more down in the hood. They're everywhere you care to look- loitering the sidewalks, on other people' s porches, abandoned porches and buildings, and in the alleyways.

Many fiends are willing to do whatever it takes to catch back that initial feeling of the very first high even to the extremes. Women are willing to give up the ass to anyone able to pay up, shit hole included in order to later get the opportunity to wrap their lips around a glass pipe and inhale. Men aren't exempt from getting sexual to get high either. Some have begged for a chance to put a dick in their mouth or get fucked in the ass for that rock. Don't get it twisted either, your neighborhood homeboy have probably got sucked off by a male dopefiend in a dark corner or basement somewhere.

But when it really gets bad for a sista on that shit, her babies are subject to getting sacrificed and put on the auction block reminiscent of slave days plus there' s no telling when the kid will get brought back home if at all. A whole bunch of crazy shit jumps off just so a fiend can get a hit of that poison.

"Girl, it is cold as hell out here and I need to score before it gets too late," a hype by the street name of Pussy, confides to her buddy. Pussy used to be a bonafide hustler back in her day strictly about paper until she allowed others in the life to influence her to just "try" drugs.

During her good days all the pimps in the city wanted to have Pussy on their team at one time or another. In her younger years she had smooth caramel colored skin, long shoulder length hair and a stroll that would make a man take a triple take. Her teeth were even and white and she sported green hued colored contacts. Her chest racked perky full breasts and the shape of her ass was similar to a basketball.

The bitch was smooth as velvet on her toes and her mouthpiece was slick as street oil. Rumors had it that she was no joke when it came to hustlin' tricks outta lettuce.

Word has it that she used to roam up and down Wisconsin Avenue and pull about twenty seventy-five dollar tricks in one day. During that time, grip like that was considered gravy money. Hell, to this day that's a nice ass stash. Nevertheless, she got up to get down. But in the midst of her hard hustling', she ended up experimenting with every type of drug available from angel dust to PCP to meth. Eventually, losing herself in the process to a dope fiend' s kryptonite and a dope man' s superpower. That shit called crack.

To look at her now you would think she was reincarnated to the likes of a bum living the hard knock life. The color of her skin now is dark and ashy looking. Her once long flowing hair is now broken off and matted down in some spots. She doesn't have enough hair on her head to even have a split end. Her titties look like flapjacks and surprisingly her ass had only shrunken down to the size of a soccer ball.

While she was scattling along down the street with her partner in getting high, Twiggy, the wind was blowing more fiercely kicking up the debris along the sidewalks. That name Twiggy was the perfect description. Twig was skinnier than Popeye the sailor man' s old girl. Sticks and skin is what you would see on first sight.

Now I can understand that some folks are born with the thin genetics but this woman was thinner than Snoop Dog. I ain't gone lie, I thought someone being smaller than him was like Tom Cruise being unable to complete a mission.

"Hold on hoe, I see that nigga's Precious car goin' toward the spot. Maybe I can hustle him up on a dick suckin' for a fifty dollar rock," she replied to Pussy.

"Bitch you oughta know damn well that P ain't about to give a scalawag like you the time of day to put your crusty ass lips on nan part of the tip of his dick," sassed Pussy.

"Awe fuck you buzzard it ain't gone hurt to try. Hell, you never know I might get lucky and if I do, don't be tryin' to wrap yo' starved for moisture deprived ass lips around the rim of my pipe, bitch. If we don't hustle for it how the hell we gone get it?" Twiggy asked.

"Hell, we both got pussies so it ain't no thang for us to go down on Third and handle some bidness but I'm tellin' you, P ain't gonna do it," Pussy informed her girl.

"Have I ever tried to knock you for doing something?" Twiggy asked her.

Pussy had to go into a brief deep thought process on that one. It didn't take her long to come up with the notion that whatever she ran by Twig on the hustle tip, Twig always had her back.

"My bad dawg. You right. I have no business knocking your hustle gurl, cuz it's my hustle too. Go do your thang chile," Pussy told her while dreaming in the back of her head how good it was gonna feel once she puffed on that pipe.

I kinda feel sorry for the zombies. I don't know and can't truly understand how folks get turned out like they do on that bullshit. Can things really get that bad? What happened to the struggle and will to survive?

Drug addicts will even sell their babies to get a hit, like Twiggy tried to do last year. Twig smoked primos (weed laced with powder) all throughout her seventh month of pregnancy. We all think she was trying to lose the baby on purpose but the little tyke was a warrior. Born two months early in a run down garage, Twig at least had the decency to put the baby in a basket and sit it on a porch of an older couple after cutting the umbilical cord with some scissors she stole from a fabric store. She cleaned the baby as best as she could with two gallons of purified water she got from the neighborhood dollar store. The outfit and blankets the baby had come from Wal-Mart's baby section that she boosted. Twig even had the decency to steal a large diaper bag and fill it up with baby bottles, diapers, wipes, rattles, a couple of pacifiers, a baby comb and brush set, baby wash and lotion, a few more outfits, socks and a couple of pair of baby shoes.

At least she had a heart in my eyes because I've heard of stories on the news of babies having been thrown in the garbage, and found dead in plastic bags.

Thank goodness the old couple down the street were generous enough to take the baby in. They knew the baby was Twiggy' s. Who could turn away a helpless baby, especially when the baby' s their grandchild?

Shit, these hypes are about to come say somethin' to me, probably hoping to suck me off for a couple of dollas or a rock.

"Hey P baaaby!" crooned Twiggy. "Look, I know you 'bout to go in and handle your functions and all but I was wonderin' if um, you and I could get together right quick yanno?"

"Get together for what Twig? You know damn well I don't get down like that, I won't disrespect myself like that yo."

I had to once again set this woman straight. Seems like every other week she propositioning me for somethin'. Gettin' some brains from a hype just really ain't my glass of Courvoiser.

Hold up! I haven't been sucked off in quite some time though. Hmmm «do I have a condom in the hooptie? Safe head is crucial, I just can't have any ol' body slobbin' on my jimmie, μ specially with all the shit goin' round nowadays.

A'ight. I deduced that I was kind of in the mood to get some brains by a headhunter, so I went on ahead and gave her a chance to drain the blood from my dick. Through a condom that is.

Hell, I initially was only gonna throw her ten dollars for the superb medulla but it was so damn good I would have been straight wrong if I didn't give her at least twelve chips. One thang is certain, a hype will slob the skin off a dick for some money to get high and I was feeling a little philanthropic today so there it is. It's a first for everything. Shit, I can put in my archives that I got some fiya ass head from a rock star. No more shame in my game. Fuck it. I only live once. Life is supposed to be about vast experiences. My nigga I was on my way to seeing before being accosted, was Loc. A hardcore cat that blew in from the Southside of Chicago, he made a name for himself here in Milwaukee. He was infamous for being a respected leader of a gang called the DOS, which stood for the Disciples of Struggle.

A lot of people misinterpreted the group of thugs for only being criminals. They helped out in the neighborhoods as best as they could. These brothers would help out the single mothers or the grandmothers who had to be mothers again because their daughters were too busy doing whatever it was that they did besides takin' care of their kids.

Don't get it twisted though, when it came time to be rowdy they were more than willing to oblige and knock a muthafucka up side the head but mainly these niggas was known for bein' boss playas: making money, spending that money, and to the right down ass broad, giving some money.

My nigga Loc had jacked up issues growing up yet he didn't allow those issues to take over his life- too much. Sure, he experimented with drugs and a lot of different women but whenever he was down, he was always able to somehow bounce back. We had had heartfelt lengthy conversations about his growing pains. If people only knew, they would have a better understanding of him besides of what they heard in the streets and from gossipers. Ignorant folks have the tendency to only talk about what they've heard instead of what they know.

Though he's a firm believer in the usage of drugs like cocaine and heroin, by looking at him you wouldn't be able to tell he ever entertained *any* type of drug. His skin wasn't discolored nor was he all scraggly looking. He stayed in a fresh whip and his lifestyle was bananas.

I suppose his drug usage was recreational. I was once told that if you used heroin once you would be addicted to it for life. Maybe I was told wrong.

Sometimes I wonder if he fucks around on the dl. I wonder that because he divulged the info to me long ago that he was molested as a child by his mother's boyfriend.

When bullshit like that happens to a small kid that experience shapes their life differently. Like BDP, I break the shits down to the very last compound on the analytical level. My hypothesis is that Loc uses the damn drugs to relieve the memories of the abuse he suffered as a shorty.

I've told the nigga more than once that ol' boy can get rolled on whenever, wherever, however. That shit is foul. Anytime a grown ass man would force a little boy to suck his jimmie and fuck him in the ass against his will needs to be dealt with in the worst way.

I would go holla at Loc every other day or so to see if I could hustle a few extra dollars making runs for him. On days when he needed me I would make about a few thousand or so in a coupla of hours at the least. Never wanting to become a fully-fledged drug dealer myself, I made a few runs here and there. The funds were proper and really I wasn't the type of cat that fit the societal description of a drug pusher even though muthafuckas knew not to fuck wit' my deranged ass ' bout my cabbage or someone I care about.

Folks still circulate the hype about me being the one that tortured a nigga for puttin' his hands on a woman I really cared about. All folks talked about was how the triflin' nigga's face was permanently rearranged. I won't say I did it, I won't say I didn't but um the fool really did need a little hood surgery done to him as far as I knew.

The severity of the surgery was equivalent to the damage he did to my friend at a distorted ratio of ten to one. Yep, he got his dirt handed back to him tenfold but later for that. Just trust and believe the mark got handled royally. I didn't do it though that was just the rumor circulated.

See, I can admit I get a little unbalanced at times. I somehow end up misplacing my marbles making it a little difficult for me to pinpoint where exactly the crystalline balls exist. I hurt too. I get gully only when necessary. At times a true gangsta just needs to make his presence felt. Feel me on that tip. Live by the sword die by the sword.

All I want to do in life is get my hustle on, stack grip, take care of my mother, meet a beautiful bitch whose wife material, marry her and get her pregnant. Getting the hustle on is fairly simple. Stackin' cheese is what I do. I make sure Moms is straight ' cuz she is the only one I have. Now the tricky part is my meeting a worthy bitch to marry and impregnate. The skeezers out here come a nickel a dozen. I may fuck around every now and then but there comes a time in a playa' s life when settling down pops up on the mental.

I learned from my mother the importance of putting away at least half of my hard hustled earnings for rainy days. You never know when some extra bread gone come in handy when you hungry or find yourself in a financial bind. I've had to dip into my stash at least twice for legal purposes. If I didn't have that bread when I needed it, I'd probably be sitting in someone' s jail right now wishing I were on the outs.

A lot of hustlers in this city make the mistake of splurgin' Big Willy style on five and ten thousand dollar rims, over priced clothes that *only* niggas will buy, jewelry and triflin' gold-diggin' hoes. All that other flashy shit draws unwanted attention like starvin' broke wannabe hustlas, stick-up kids, and heat from the pigs.

Hold up though, ain't nothin' wrong with splurgin' on hoes every now and then but yanno what I'm sayin'.

One thing about hoes is that there' s no chance for misunderstandings. A whore will get paid to handle whore business and there won't be any strings attached. Everyone gets satisfied and can go on about life as usual.

Peep game. There are two kinds of triflin' hoes: the first one being the upfront only out to get in yo' pockets type. This type of broad will let you know in a New York minute that to fuck with her you gotta drop them duckets. Then the other, who' ll play the good bitch frontin' role until she gets your nose open, when upon that happening, she'll break your ass off in so many places you wouldn't be able to tell if God really did put your shit hole in the right place type of hoe when shit gets ugly. That's the kind of bitch that will definitely fuck with your boys behind your back. A mental black eye in the game all round. At least with the first hoe you already know what her agenda is, with the second one a playa has to stay on his p' s and q' s.

Now I can't forget about another kind of hoe. Actually, this type of hoe has goals in life but in order to achieve those goals she has to get down for hers. I can never knock a hustler like that. I can see myself getting down with a hoe like this last one.

I'm the type of man that's attracted to go-getters. I can't see myself fuckin' with a funky ass bitch that ain't ' bout shit. It just ain't in me to allow a punk bitch to fade the color off my drawers unless I make certain she broke me off somethin' proper while I was fuckin' with her.

Gotta stay strong in the battlefield like a Trojan and keep a serious eye for checkin' change. No time for hoochie games. Momma always told me only one bitch made me. Her. And she also told me to never to let a bitch break me …mentally, physically or fiscally.

Rat Qualities

I had plans this weekend to treat LaQuanda to a weekend of bliss. I can't help messing with her, that killa pussy is astronomical. Stars, meteorites, constellations, and unidentified flying objects, hell, the whole universe is what I end up seeing after boning her.

Am I whipped? Nah, but why would a sane man deliberately decline some bonafide killa pussy? Love? Hell nawl! Well I do know that's certainly not the case with her. I know for a fact, she's diggin' me too because my skills between, under and even without the sheets rate a solid ten on the Richter scales. I dick a bitch down hard and sweet.

I just don't know how long this sex relationship will last because sometimes I think I'm just about ready to find a quality woman to spend my time with. I need to improve on how I play my cards with these broads though cuz Karma is a mutha. It'll be just my luck that I run into a girl I really end up liking and get dogged the fuck out.

I have my frolicky flings, associates, interest calls whatever you wanna call it. I might care to tear an asshole up or get my dick sucked from time to time. All men do. I gotta keep those type of broads on my line. The only feelings involved consist of the sensations that occur when I'm about to bust and the aftermath of washing my shit up to raise up out the spot. Like Snoop Dogg, I don't love dem hoes.

LaQuanda is what one would consider a jumpdown. She's a three f-er: flirt, feed and get to fuck. It's a four to five step program. Smile at her ass. Give her the googly eyes. Take her for a meal at your nearest neighborhood spot. If you're feeling good throw in a movie. Finally, finish her off at a cheap room somewhere.

Hoodrats give up the ass quick and some know how to give exceptional brains. They only need to be treated like a lady one time for it to be on and poppin'. I couldn't invest any quality time or feeling in a rat. Too much work. I could go out to any club in the city and end up seeing the same broads all of them damn near looking the same, wearing damn near identical outfits.

I consider a quality woman to have some game about herself and how she lives life. This type of woman won't have three kids by five different niggas. Yall know the type, one kid' s father is questionable because she had downed two or three different playas within the same time frame and the tests haven't been confirmed yet. The other two are for sure fathers cuz when she was fucking with them she wasn't fucking around.

To meet a broad with no kids at all is a winning punch out the gate. I don't think I want a readymade family. I want to make a family. And besides, I'm not tryin' to bust a cap in a nigga over some stupid shit because most broads fuck with the baby daddy every now and then.

When I meet a woman who doesn't have any kids automatically clues me in on a few things about that situation. For one, she's very cautious when she gets down. Two, she's not foolish enough to get caught up barefoot, pregnant and lonely by just any ol' cat. Three, she's abortion prone. And lastly, she could just be waiting until her situation is airtight before settling down like that.

A quality woman for my taste wouldn't prefer smoking weed for breakfast, lunch and dinner or drinking alcohol everyday to doing something to better herself and her situation. Shit, my type of woman wouldn't sport weaves of seriously unnatural colors like that red hot fire shit unless its for a hair show or the white as lightning blondes with nails hanging as long as the talons on an eagle with all of that 3D gunky sparkly shit on them. That's just a little too damn ghetto fab for me.

Now don't get me wrong, some ghetto looking ass broads are righteous and down as hell but all that flamboyant shit gots to go. Some naturalness *is* truly appreciated. Some women just try too damn hard to get some attention. I'm really attracted to classy women with flava'.

The life of a playa ain't all that damn easy. Slangin' dick between every set of legs that open up has landed a bruh in the clinic once upon a time. I've been burnt before and that embarrassing ass shit taught my black ass a lesson that won't ever be forgotten. Imagine needing to piss really bad like you've been drinking a twelve pack of beer within an hour or something. Three seconds into the piss, a horrible body crippling sensation of porcupine pins and intense unbelievable heat come out. A nigga was on *fiya*! I don't know what the heat feels like when a volcano erupts but hell I'd like to bet that it's close to what I felt. Then to top it off, my groin area was prickly and itchin' something crazy. Probably like termites chewin' on some wood. I had a double whammy put on me.

Shoulda kept my mind on some money instead of seeking a nut. But believe me, the bitch was mystifying. She had the face, small waist *and* the big bubble ass. I just had to rip that. Just had to. I didn't know she was the neighborhood hoe though. BBD always sang don't trust a big ol' ass and a smile. Shoulda did my research. That was all my bad. I know I don't ever want to land that incurable package. I need to live life to the fullest so condoms stay on the dick, even when I'm sleep at a broad' s crib.

A quality woman for my taste is a boss bitch. A smart getting down for her' s type of bitch by any means necessary book and street wise. She' d be good-lookin' with a bangin' ass body and a style all of her own. A playa gets tired of seeing women in skin- tight jeans with the surplus midriff hanging over the top of the pants. Skid marks on the stomach from not moisturizing during the developing stages of pregnancy, weight gain or loss, or the kind of ass without a shape at all- wide, flat and sloppy looking (noassitol).

A woman who takes care to take care of herself may very well take damn good care of me too.

No copycattin' allowed. My quality woman won't be   looking' like every other broad in the city either, clothes, hair, or style-wise. She'll have her own personal style. For the life of me I don't understand why everyone cares to look like everybody else. Or why bitches believe they can look like Beyonce with the horse' s hair down to the ass when in reality they   looking' like "Umfoofu" or a "Boochichi."

Why do hoodrats think they standin' on shit wearing that knockoff gear? Or why do some of them wear that cheap ass cluster diamond jewelry? I can't stand no fake, stank, or broke hoe. And if necessary a hoe that can't hoe. Now if she got the qualities I require then she can have me. She gots to be a smooth, classy-stunting on the highest level type of bitch. Plus at the same time down for a muthafucka like me.

It's hard being in these streets tryin' to figure out whose down for you and who ain't. Sometimes I don't know who to trust that's why I only deal with a select few. Fuck those rabbit ass hoes. On tha real.

Making Runs

My nigga Loc had needed me to run on 28th Auer Street to pick up some money that was ready for him. Being that I was only less than five minutes away from there, I didn't anticipate it taking me that long to handle that business.

When I got there I noticed trouble already in the making. Arriving on the block, all I saw were police cars and people looking out their windows and standing on their top porches being nosy. Black folks know they can be nosy when some shit jump off.

So I parked down the street and waited in my whip to watch things unfold. Peeping two unmarked detective cars and three squads parked up and down the street I knew something foul had to have happened. Problem is I didn't see anybody outside. It was like a straight up ghost town. When the peoples come ' round folks get scarce.

A dark blue unmarked car was sitting down the street that I knew was driven by this dirty, crooked ass detect who enveloped a name fit for a pussy. At this point in the game, I weighed my options on whether or not I was game to take a chance and get that bread from the house I was supposed to go to or miss out on some easy scratch. It didn't take long for me to figure that shit out either. A playa layed in the cut considering the circumstances.

Ten minutes later, I saw the pigs taking a young stud out shirtless and in handcuffs from the spot where I was supposed to go. I immediately recognized that detective.

They call this mark, Brunette. Brunette' s one of many dirty detectives in Milwaukee that rob dope dealers, run game on them and threaten to kill them if word ever got out about it. I know hustlers that have been sweated out they grip. Nevermind the bogus police report that was never filed. Regardless of the amount change a dealer would have on their person to take they would still get taken to jail on a trumped up charge such as a petty warrant or outstanding parking tickets.

There' s simply no way a police detective can afford to live in a three hundred thousand dollar house, have options to drive either a black or white Corvette on city salary and sport tailor made suits on the daily with Gucci loafers on the feet. Well, only if the wife is loaded and that is simply not the case.

Research was conducted involving his background as well as a few others.

Corruption rules this city but it is always the brothers going to jail and prison.

In the drug trade the higher uppers know damn well that black folks don't drop the dope off the planes or ride it in on the boats nevertheless it's the white boys that hardly ever serves a day in jail.

City officials skim the taxpayers of hundreds of thousands of dollars and don't serve a day in jail. But let a brother or sista put a move down and cash a check or somethin' and they asses going straight to jail or prison, fuck probation. White folks don't even get probation, they get to participate in some bullshit "I learned from my mistake" counseling class and a punk ass fine for the crimes they do. Ain't thatta bitch?

The boys in the hood had to either pay Brunette off or face the consequences of getting set up, found stankin' or catching a serious ass federal case that could ultimately send them to prison serving twenty-five to life sentences on some conspiracy shit. The great land of America huh? Yea ok.

I backed up immediately and stormed back to Loc' s place and it's a good thing I did because he had absolutely no clue as to what was shakin' on the block. Apparently, the young hustler didn't even get the opportunity to warn him.

"Yo Loc, shit ain't lookin' too right over there on Auer," I told him while putting my keys in my pocket.

"Man I ain't heard from none of my peeps in the past half hour and you know damn well I always hear from them nuts," he informed me.

"Yea, I rolled up over there like you needed and when I pulled around the corner I noticed that the neighborhood was as vacant as an eagle flying thru the desert. I knew shit wasn't quite right when I peeped the unmarked detect cars. So I waited until I was able to see and low and behold that crooked-ass muthafucka Brunette was escorting one of the peeps out in handcuffs."

"Man, that gotdamn pig needs to be blown off the face of this earth. He only sweats the hood but those white boys over in Germantown and Pewaukee never get sweated and they floodin' the city with that X and heroin."

"Yo, word is he's on someone' s bankroll out there to make sure heat never catches out that way but some Mexicans down on the south have a price of a hundred stacks on his head," I informed Loc.

"Now that shit is steep 'cuz them taco eatin' muthafuckas play no games when it comes to this drug shit, they will roast a pig on a bonfire and the illest thang is no one will ever be able to figure out who dun it," Loc joked.

"Dude, we need some cats like that on our squad for real. But who' s to say they won't turn on our black asses one day?" I asked.

"Mexicans only have true loyalty amongst themselves man, and I know I wouldn't want to be found rotten."

"I know dawg I know. Truthfully, if I had some contacts to get in good with them I'll fuck with them," he answered, "plus I could probably get a much better tag and product than what I been getting from the niggas in Cali."

Upon learning the news from me on what was shakin' in the hood he closed shop and bounced to make a few runs. He had to make sure everything was on the smooth cuz rats in the Mil kick it in packs.

Damn, that change of plans fucked up my change. It pays to have a back up plan at all costs when shit goes haywire.

I now figured I should go pay a visit to a pimp buddy of mine named Onyx. He had a string of hoes working for him cross- country. And when I say cross-country I mean just that ...cross- country.

Onyx put his hoes on the hoe strips of Chicago, Detroit, New York and Vegas. His spot at home was down on Wisconsin Avenue five minutes from downtown Milwaukee. His women would work twenty-four hour days ho' n that money up. I'm not talkin' chump change either, each broad of his would bring him no less than one thousand a day like clockwork.

That's a lot of humpin' and suckin' to do in Milwaukee. But what got to be done got to be done. When he takes his troops to the strips of Vegas, he sets the quota at two thousand per day.

It took me about fifteen minutes to get there ' cause my hooptie wouldn't go too fast but it gets me where I need to go. Shit, when its winter and the wind is cold enough to make your bottom lip split when you smile, you know its time to break out the petroleum jelly, wool socks and thermal wear.

I copped this car from an older person who just had it sitting in the back yard for years getting all rusty and shit. The old playa sold it to me for only sixteen hundred and I've grown attached to it. Hell, I even named the ol' girl Lilly. Yep, it just be me and my Lilly roamin' the streets handling functions.

There' s something incredibly reliable about old school Chevys. It's no secret that those cars were built to last past your death back in the day. Nowadays, these plastic ass cars rule the streets. I mean damn, anytime you can simply kick a car and the dent fall right back out you know you've just entered into the twilight zone. With my car, I can run through a fleet of those plastic cars and damage will be at the max, a broken headlight.

A lot of old heads like the old school cars so much that they' ll have an old beat up car completely restored both mechanically and physically. Now the young studs prefer not to have all original shit in the car and opt out instead to have boomin' sound systems installed and those expensive five and ten thousand dollar rims on them. Then they go and get the flippin' or bowling ball paint jobs that run about four thousand or more all depending on which rip off shop does it.

A playa like myself prefers to keep it simple and on the low. A lot of flossin' can be detrimental to a playa' s livelihood. I know plenty of hustlers that have been murdered by the game due to fucking with some drugs they had no business fucking with, dealin' with a lot of different women or from the jealousy of the amount of money they were clockin'.

Since x hit the scene, these cats be lost in space. Ecstasy is damn near the new crack of today for younger folks.

Hoes that work in the clubs would look good as hell one month then from fucking with x a few months down the line they look beat up and tired. And then before you know it their price for the pussy goes on the decline. One hoe in the club, Butter, used to tax two hundred for the ass. Since being on that x the tag is now just a mere seventy-five dollars.

Damn.

The Dame

Precious was only twenty-eight but he's been in the streets damn near all his life so he's seen and come across just about everything there is to come across. He earned his phd (pimpin' hoes degree) from his mother whose street name was Blue.

Blue was the number one prostitute in the city at one time back in the day. Being a vet and all she's earned her stripes and is still commanding shit to this day like a general commands his army. With connects to judges, high priced attorneys and politicians her operation runs unscathed in the city.

Basically, no one fucks with her even if they thought they could. Trying to fuck in her business could cause personal havoc. You' d think she was the last don or something. She never even acquired a parking ticket during her hustle. She had that juice.

Street history has it that as she got older, she decided to put her own pimpin' down and gathered up some young girls to put them to work in hoe houses and on the track. The girls she normally came up with were either homeless or had gotten pregnant and their parents kicked them out.

Her game plan was to find gals with low self-esteem issues, groom them and turn them out into money chasers. The philosophy was when you saw a potential trick chase his ass down.

As popular as Blue was it would have been hard to not have heard of her, but quite a few of the girls did through the grapevine finding out that she's a female captain of sorts. A few of them needed to get on the grind with Blue's guidance which would have been better than hooking up with a finesse or gorilla pimp.

Finesse pimps were the pretty boys of the game with the perfectly coiffed hair, manicured nails, expensive clothes and smooth silky game. The gorillas on the other hand laid hands on or feet in their hoes. They were the kind that stomped their bitches down having no problems torturing them for any kind of so-called infraction. Violations were considered to be acts of treason to the pimp: looking some other pimp in the eyes; speaking when not spoken to; not bringing in the daily quota and some other shit. Some of the girls really had no choice considering the various predicaments they were in for fucking with one.

Either way, once hooking up with the Queen Bitch they no longer had to worry about where they were gonna get their next meal or any beatings.

If the broads didn't have clothes, it wasn't a thang to Blue cuz she had a bonafide squad of boosters who would go into any store on any avenue and wreck shop. Boosters were on file that could misappropriate whatever gear ordered from the cheaper shit found in the neighborhood malls to the expensive shit like Gucci or Prada found on the racks of boutiques on the Magnificent Mile.

Nevertheless, Blue wasn't the charity army just out saving hoes and all, the broads had to put in due diligence to live under her. And that meant sharing ass with the world.

The Luring

Back in her early days Blue was persuaded to get in the hoe game by a smooth talking, handsome cat called Fox, a finesse type nigga.

She was only sixteen when he started to swoo her with flowers, dinners and clothes. Her mother didn't want her fucking with the nigga but considering herself of being almost grown, she went against those wishes. Eventually, Blue left her home to get with Fox and was slowly introduced into the game of pimping and whoring.

At that time, Fox was in his early twenties when he caught sight of Blue walking home from school one day. He had his own roof over his head crushed out with nice velvet furniture and curtains, thick red carpets and two big 38-inch screen televisions.

In those days a young black man living like that was considered to be trumpin' in a sort. Fox even rolled around in big old school Cadillacs with the wide white trimmed tires, every black man's dream ride.

He made certain that Blue stayed laced in the best when she went to school. Dressed in Jordache, Valentino and Calvin Klein the young, chocolate stallion was the envy of many a hoe. Girls would wonder and whisper amongst themselves about how she looked every day plus the amount of money she pulled out everyday in the lunchroom buying lunch.

Not every young high schooler can go into their pockets or purses and yank out a small roll of fives, tens and twenties. Betta believe she wasn't pulling her grip out of a cheap ass pocketbook either. The gal had Louis Vuittons, MCMs and Coach bags. Teachers weren't even able to cop that shit on the salaries they made therefore many had questions as how the young girl they knew as Millicent Black could.

Several teachers had all but participated in short sighted speculations about the way certain students looked and behaved. The mystery to them about Millicent involved questions concerning whether or not her parents had money or if she was involved in any kind of illegal activity.

Money was not ever an issue with Blue cuz her man kept her. Every once in a while he took her shopping in Chicago to the more upscale stores where a designer t-shirt could cost bank and logo jeans ran about sixty dollars. Blue was sporting Coco Chanel, Liz Claiborne, and Vertigo as well as Burberry way before these times.

Milwaukee stores didn't know shit about shit when it came to fashion until it was late. You' d think it was a country ass city.

The broads at the school had no fashion sense either until they saw the threads in a fashion magazine wishing they could afford the expensive clothes.

All this shopping and splurging was the prelude. He knew he had to reel her in somehow and what young girl doesn't like nice clothes, shoes, purses and made to feel special? Little did Blue know, but Fox had other goals for her to achieve when the time was right.

Time went on and eventually Fox sat Blue down and questioned her loyalty to him.

"Princess, we've been together for a little while now and I need to know how you feel about me because I know already that I have deep, deep feelings for you. I've also shown you how much I care for you and your well-being and you ought to know by now that I only have your best interests at heart. Do you understand that?" he finally asked her.

She replied, "Yes I understand. I know you care about me because if you didn't you wouldn't do the things that you've done and are doing for me. I never had a man in my life until you came along and I'm loyal to you in more ways than just one baby."

"Being that that's the case, we need to take this relationship of ours to the next level. And on this level, Princess, respect will always be given and I trust that it will be equally returned. In order for it to work it must be mutual. I don't want you to ever think that I could care less for you or think any less of you for what I'm about to put on the table for you to think about, but what I would like for you to do would not only help *us* more financially but would also bring *us* closer to each other, you feeling me Baby?"

"You are like the father I never had and my choice is to be with you, so what do you want to ask me about?" she inquired.

Blue' s biological father was murdered in a gambling house on Chicago' s Westside when she was just six years old. So her mother had to make shit happen for the two of them. It's probably where Blue got her hustling genes from.

Fox laid out the principles of dancing and getting paid for sex to his lady. At first Blue wondered how he could even ask her to sleep with other men for money when she was just a virgin upon meeting him. She gave herself to him willingly and now he wanted her to share herself with complete strangers. She immediately got past those reservations.

In Blue' s world there was no need for questioning. She loved her nigga. He was the first man she' d ever been with that showered her with affection, gifts and most of all, attention. He encouraged her to do well in school. He kept her laced with the finest. He made certain that she ate well like the rich and famous: lobster tails and exotic seafood that was unfathomable to most struggling blacks in those days. He sported her around town in his black on black Cadillac making sure all the other studs in the city knew that she was his woman, front and center. He even had to go so far as to stand on a few cats necks about tryin'to fuck with her disrespectfully.

Make no mistake, the love he had for her was obvious. Now it was time for Blue to show him the extent of her love. Strange? Yes. Necessary? Yes. Moral? Who knows and if they do, who can judge?

In Fox' s world, he never came across someone with the triple threat-beauty, brains and bangin' ass body.

Blue stood tall like a gazelle on muscular, shapely legs with an ass like the shape of a basketball. Her breasts were fully shaped with roundness of medium sized grapefruits followed by a smooth, flat contoured midriff. Her blooming skin complexion shone a pellucid deep mahogany brown along with her face possessing the eyes of an exotic Siamese cat. She appeared to be something of a phenomenon. The hands and feet on her body were delicate.

The choice hairstyle at that time was the Afro and Blue' s Afro was large, thick and jet black, which on some days she wore with a headband. Two words truly described her …ethereal goddess. So of course, he was smitten with her beauty.

Naturally, he had fucked around with the hoodrats but the maturity level of those very rodents was null and void. All those skanks wanted to do was skip school, fuck and get high everyday. No type of direction at all.

To be seen with a good looking sire like himself, coupled with the reputation of getting lettuce was not only the icing on the cake but the delectable ice cream topping as well.

He became so weary of inadvertently *having* to fuck with the lames that he forwent all the pussy catapulted at him on the daily and made the conscious decision to not be hounded and concentrate more on just Millicent.

Recognize that the pussy available to him was in vast abundance therefore he had to be serious about his girl to not want to have any unnecessary extra relations.

So on that note, he hustled each and every day stackin' his produce. At times, he wasn't even able to call his woman for being so damn busy. Being that he didn't use the narcotics he sold or any of its cousins he was able to stay on his square at all times and keep his pharmacy well supplied.

Peeping game from all levels of street life he made concrete, loyal contacts simultaneously garnering a small but thorough legion of executioners available for the dirty work when necessary. Fox wasn't the type of young stud who would wild out when shit pissed him off. He was far more calculating than that. A plan had to be put in motion to get rid of any threatening archenemies. Hence, he didn't spend more money than he made and he kept his promissory notes locked away safely in safe deposit boxes and buried in yards throughout Milwaukee and Chicago.

He was even resourceful about the manner he kept his money. Instead of leaving it in cash, he bought vast amounts of safety money orders from the check cashing businesses in the hood. In case anything janky were to happen to him the peoples couldn't just up and take his cold cash. Self-preservation in the game is necessary or else.

With the love of a good woman comes the unparallel devotion of someone willing, able and ready to do anything for her man. Strong men need strong women.

In Blue' s senior year, she went against Fox' s wishes and dropped out of school to start dancing. Don't get it twisted, Fox wanted her to get fast money but he also wanted her to be smart and finish high school first.

His main desire was to turn his hustle money into business money so they could live off of it without any repercussions. He made his chips off the streets of the ghetto, selling vial after vial of the dope called cocaine and bag after bag of cannabis plus any other kind of drug that could induce hallucinations like THC. He couldn't spell or read that damn well but that nigga could count money backwards and multiply it a hundred times to come up with a nasty equation equivalent to financial success.

As time progressed, Fox took his dame on tour to different states to get down. He was initially against the idea of his jewel dropping out of school to become street property but Blue was determined to not work a nine to five for vittles.

Envy

When a woman' s mind is made up …it's made up.

Hoe money was good money especially when tallied up at the end of the night.

Blue first began her newfound profession in downtown Chicago on Rush Street having raked up five hundred a day. Before long, she went all over to the tracks of Memphis, Atlanta, Jersey, Charlotte, Fort Wayne and Miami. Loving the fast money, she would hustle up more than three thousand a week consistently.

Knowing that she had the love of Fox on her side she hustled even harder. She was no dummy though, she got her own safe deposit box and by the time she was almost nineteen she accumulated more than $70,000 in savings.

She reciprocated Fox' s generosity and bought him expensive clothes and designer shoes from Bernini' s in Chicago and Viaggio' s in Milwaukee. No woman had ever bought Fox now-n-later gators with a crisp cashmere suit to match so she was the first. Blue wanted to do for her man what he did for her. She even bought him a five-carat diamond ring VS class so that whenever he gazed upon it he would be certain to think of the thoroughbred that put it on his finger. She didn't have him just bling- blingin', she had her nigga crunchy. Little did she know, Fox was never going to forget her.

Yea, he knew that she was saving bread in her own box. He knew she loved him wholeheartedly, that's why he entrusted her with the knowledge of his stash in any event something was to ever happen to him. He wanted her to have it. Not his family or so- called friends.

Hell, his perpetrating buddies thirsted to have Blue for themselves but see, she recognized game when it was attempted to be played. The niggas would have to drop major grip to fuck with her, as a dutiful wife she would gladly give the change directly to her husband.

Jealously set in niggas heads throughout Milwaukee and a plot was devised to off him. One night while Fox was in traffic, a blue Chevy pulled along side of his ' Lac and unleashed a brigade of bullets leaving him filled with eight bullets. Thing is, the occupants of the blue Chevy screeched off before checking to see if their target was annihilated.

Fox always kept a bulletproof vest on him especially while on the hustle. Five of the bullets lodged themselves in the vest while three spliced through his flesh in his left arm and leg. He drove himself to the hospital over on Burleigh Street.

Being that all gunshot wounds have to be reported to the police he made certain to remove the vest and stash it in the bushes by the hospital before going in to get stitched up.

He already knew that niggas in the streets were envious of him ballin' out of control. Having an idea already of who it could've been that put him in the ICU unit, he set a plan in motion to wage war. His own assassins were to lay in wait and watch their prey for a few weeks before making a move. Frontin' on him will soon cause muthafuckas in the Mil to meet his soldiers from the windy city.

Weeks later the ambush was planned and executed flawlessly. Chi-town niggas don't leave evidence and they certainly don't leave witnesses behind to tell any stories. The punks in that blue Chevy were dealt with royally. The punks of opposition were bound, gagged, tied and tortured mercilessly in a broke down garage on the east side of town. The gruesome murders were reported on all the news stations for two weeks straight.

This case was more than difficult for the pigs because fingers had been severed; teeth had been extracted; heads had been decapitated; penises dislodged and eyes were gauged out of the skulls. Which made it extremely baffling for the pigs to figure out.

Assholes wanted to shine like him, grind like him, fuck that beautiful broad like him but they would never be the Fox. They would never have the chance. Evil thoughts had no choice but to run and take residence in his heart and mind. Revenge ultimately was his in the end.

"Those fools tried to send me to the pearly gates but like roaches, I ain't eligible for dying," he thought to himself. Getting gully was a favorite past time for him little did niggas really know.

"Don't these muthafucks know I'll have no recourse but to become a menace to their society tryin' to fuck in my business?" he asked himself out loud.

"They really must've wanted parts of me and now they can't even think cuz their heads are crushed up somewhere. If they could think they would be like "Damn, Fox straight shitted on us," he laughed to himself. "Muthafuckas betta play they part and recognize I'm not that nigga to fuck wit' ! And they sho' as all of flaming hell betta not fuck with my woman cuz if they do, I'm coming for they family-mammas, sistas, brothas, nieces, nephews, aunts, uncles, any living grandparents, bitch ass baby mammas and they kids," he roared. The madness had begun. Evil pervaded Fox' s mind and in turn created a maniac.

Now you know damn well people that think like that don't have good sense and are definitely not in the right frame of mind. Marbles are totally lost at this point. The chips are stacked on both shoulders and any time some of those chips leaving is unforeseeable. That is another book though. Fox survived the battle streets but hereditary malignant cancer caught up with him destroying his body and mind at a feverish pace. At the young age of twenty-seven he succumbed to the grim reaper leaving the love of his life behind.

Survival

Blue was left to fend for herself but she had a great mentor and knew now that it was for her to become the captain of her own ship.

Out of respect for her first and only man, she refused to fuck with the nothing ass niggas in the streets. Many small time hustlers came at her from all angles with all types of game but she was steadfast in her decision. No man alive would or could ever take the place of Fox in her heart. A true love is hard to come by and it doesn't wither away despite time.

Blue went to the secret stash spot Fox had shown her and secured his money along with hers. The next day she made the decision to enroll back in classes down at the community college. It wasn't necessary for her to hustle the streets being that she had over three hundred thousand to hold her over until she could make some legal shit happen the way she wanted it to happen.

She meticulously hid the money and watched her back for the vultures that instead of flying, walked about her.

Her first step was to enroll in the technical college downtown but attend classes at one of the far out locations and finish her high school diploma. That very same year she took up college courses until she came across the idea of making money in real estate.

Leaving the technical college for another gamble she decided to research real estate classes.

Her research landed information pertaining to the costs of taking the classes at one of the major real estate businesses. The fees were minimal.

Upon learning the real estate game, she ventured out and invested in a couple of cheap city houses and rehabilitated them.

In her first year she bought three houses, one was for her to live in and the other two she rented out. She turned her duplex into a two story one family house decked out with marble and hardwood floors, custom made leather furniture and all the amenities of the rich and famous.

The second year she copped three more city houses and made those into boarding houses that turned out more than twenty three hundred a month. During the third year of her being in the real estate game she bought two more duplexes and made those into whorehouses.

Copping property at this rate, Blue concluded that she didn't have to sell her ass or dance anymore to make amends. With time, good credit and business acumen she was able to spend her money as she wished. She was the only young black woman in the city with a white on white Range Rover and a 600LS. Luxury living was what she was used to with Fox and living the luxury life was the only way she could foresee herself living out the rest of her life. Being a shrewd and calculating businesswoman catapulted her into a society many hustling blacks dreamed of.

At the age of twenty-six Blue she stood at five feet nine with a cocoa brown complexion. Her ass was so huge it would have taken three hands just to cup one of her ass cheeks. Her breasts were the size of oranges and she had a small waist. To be in her thirties, this woman could still walk rings around the young girls she ran and cop more scrilla than them all put together. She got the name Blue because no matter what she wore, she had the color blue on somewhere in the ensemble.

Blue had a number of houses throughout the city full of ample, succulent young whores whose main mission in life or rather only mission in life was to make money. Some of the girls came into the game because they were neglected, sexually abused, mentally castrated and/or physically harmed. The young girls coming from those kinds of homes didn't care one way or the other that they had to sell their essence as long as there was a light at the end of the dark tunnel they had been previously living in.

Blue indulged the gals to "princess" pampering after work was put in treating them to experiences they've never even fathomed like full spa ministrations that consisted of aromatherapy pedicures and manicures followed by scented paraffin wax dips, fully body massages, seaweed body wraps and intricately designed hairdos. Once a month, Blue took the girls on shopping expeditions in the more upscale malls of Illinois.

Many of the girls who worked for the Dame adored this woman who was more of a mother to them than the wombs they sprouted from. Loyalty was expected of every one of the girls. Strange as it reads, none of the girls had problems with making thousands of dollars and handing it over this woman. Major pimpin'. While a so-called gorilla had to beat a broad to make her stay with him or had to consistently take on the role of a babysitter to make their broad pay them, these young girls flocked to Blue's nest and conversation was paramount.

Broken promises were never in Blue's repertoire.

This woman was a woman of her word and with each syllable spoken. She stood on what she said to the fullest.

The young girls that came into contact with her immediately saw the thoroughness of the older lady making the choice to fuck with her swift and accurate.

Pussy is power. Pussy is a hot commodity. Pussy is a necessity to the heterosexual that is. Pussy is money. Pussy is a business.

Trick Conception

Precious was the product of this type of work. His father was a white regular who was in town on business when he had dealings with Blue, which was every other week.

A condom broke during a late night tryst and the trick' s semen manifested inside of Blue' s anatomy. Blue decided to keep her whoreson instead of running to the abortion clinic. The bed was made and she had no qualms about lying in it. The trick had no clue that he helped create a beautiful son that would eventually come into the business of supplying what he paid earnestly and faithfully for.

The single mother didn't think twice on whether or not to tell the biological father of their son because she thought that   he would discontinue their working business relationship furthermore, the trick was married. He had a lot to lose if the shit ever hit the fan and yet she gained everything. Alone.

Precious never had a father in his life so he had to learn survival skills from his sole parent. Blue taught her baby boy the lessons of life instilling principles of the boomerang. Whatever you throw out will eventually come back to you, the Law of Karma. She made certain to teach her prized pupil to respect and revere women no matter what their chosen lifestyle was. Precious also learned the dark side of the streets from his mother. Sugarcoating shit wasn't her forte, she always handed her lessons to her son in the raw, upfront and personal. Since he didn't have a father he learned even more grimy shit from the hustlers in the streets that took him under their wings.

Sure, he could have walked the straight and narrow road but the compelling lure of the streets beckoned him. Not that the calling was difficult for him to hear because he had street blood coursing through his thin veins. Hell, he was a trick baby so he went to what called him naturally.

Caught Pimp

Precious grew up to be a smooth operator who made the wiser choice in not associating with the other pimps in the city too much. He saw that the other pimps were far too flamboyant with their business and only desired diamonds, furs, and cars while carrying around those cheap rhinestone encrusted goblets. He had yet to witness a pimp with a genuine diamond decorated cup.

That shit was considered cool in the pimp game but unwarranted attention isn't for everyone.

The peoples like to get in the business of backtracking all your info from when you were born, to the schools you ever attended, churches visited, info on family members to even the folks you meet and greet everyday. Getting caught up for pimping and pandering isn't a good charge. Therefore, he opted to keep a low profile.

Precious drove a ' 69 Cadillac Eldorado that still had the original factory equipment in it. He also wore everyday clothes like jeans, shirts and sweaters. He wasn't into the lite-brite suits and gators garb unless it was a holiday.

It's not difficult to catch a case for pimping and pandering. All someone had to do was put the people in the trade and it's on from there. In some instances like those the initiator is a family member of the girl getting pimped on that actually cares. Those occasions are rare.

One pimp got caught out there for fuckin' on a little girl. He did the r and b move. This guy was so dirty that he and his main woman would have all kinds of sex with the young gal including anal relations. The poor girl didn't have anyone who gave a damn about her to rescue her from the monsters. Word is that this young gal was fourteen and her mother was a dope addict. The pimp was her first sexual encounter.

When it's all said and done, men love young untouched tenders. With some distorted guidance, the girl learned every sexual trick existent to man to then only learn to perfect other tricks on women just as well. Rumor was the young girl could deep throat nine inches without gagging and her pussy could stretch far enough to fit a fist in it.

When the pimp got caught up he was sent to prison for twenty years for kidnapping and sexual assault of a minor. His main bitch was sentenced to fifteen. That ain't nearly enough time for fucking with an underage girl like that. The mental scars from that abuse can last a lifetime.

Expectations

Precious had dreams of becoming a successful hood real estate mogul like his mother. He figured why go to college for four plus years to not be guaranteed a job when he could study real estate for six months and get much richer much quicker.

His mother went on to become a real estate broker in the business. From her education in the books and in the streets she had erudite the art of buying old abandoned homes, investing five thousand or more into them and either reselling to the highest bidders or making her money right back with the girls living and working out of the homes. Not bad for a woman who didn't finish high school on time. Hard work and perseverance paid off in the long run after all. That's how Precious was able to live the comfortable life.

Many prostitutes in the game were either doped out or were being pimped by the flashy cats. There's many a women who get into the sport for the fame who end up having nothing to show for being in the game down the line. Dumb whores.

I know hoes that have clocked fifty grand easy part-time to still be ridin' on a bus with no stable living arrangements. These same hoes would rather up they money to a pimp so he can floss the best threads and roll on those dubs showing off all the jewelry.

Then on the flip side, there are those rare hoes that have their heads on straight and use their hard hustled money to take care of business like school, mortgages, vehicle notes and their own rich desires. It's hard for a pimp to check grip with those kind of broads. The so-called great "pimp" conversation ultimately ends up appearing wack and lacking strength.

Single parents can be good influences for their children as long as their heads are on tight. From Blue, Precious was able to see firsthand the versatility his mother possessed and how she utilized her skills to reach full potential.

Onyx always tried to get me interested in the game even though I made a promise to myself to not ever get involved. Dealing with a lot of different broads can be taxing on a bruh' s mental, all the whinin' and cacklin' would make me snap out.

"Say man, you should quit bullshittin' and get down with this hoe game. It's all very simple like I done told you. Get a gang of hoes and get your riches," he impressed upon me.

"When the dope game fails you, hoe money won' t, pussy is always up for auction," Onyx lectured.

"Man I'm beginning to feel everything you been sayin' dog. Loc had to close up shop today and I missed out on some much needed change," I told him.

Truthfully, I haven't really entertained the thought of dealing with different broads and their funny ass attitudes on a daily basis. I've been around enough to know how women can be with each other. When they all on their periods and in the same vicinity it ain't no joke. Then there' s all the whimpering when they want shit. But hell, promises are made to be broken and since I didn't promise this shit to myself in a blood ritual I gotta do what I gotta do. Now if I did dive off into that profession, I wouldn't have to worry about how and where I would be getting my girls, ' cause Onyx had that on lock for me. It shouldn't be a problem for me to get started with a couple of moneymakers and catch grip. If the dope games ever cease, pussy will always sell. Always.

Tricks cruisin' the streets of Milwaukee would pay at least seventy- five dollars to be serviced by one of Blue's girls. Shit, that was only good for a hand or blowjob. Granted, if the sensations felt from that were enticing enough to the trick, he could probably pay an additional fee of the same range and get fucked senseless for about five to ten.

Normally, if the atmosphere of the street was too busy or gritty, a trick could opt out to get handled at one of the houses where it was more comfortable and more private. A trip like that would run the mark about one hundred fifty smacks upfront.

All kinds of clientele visited the whorehouses on the regular. Even stars came through once in a while to get sucked and fucked. There was money to be made, money to be spent and money to be tricked. The true money chasers were like bloodhounds game for hunting dead presidents down.

Onyx' s mom had turned a few tricks every once in a while just to have that extra cash on hand when she had to deal with bullshit ass temporary jobs that weren't paying her enough bread to buy crackers. Hell, when times got tense his mother got down for her crown.

I used to overhear conversations in the street from old heads how she usta make tricks bust in less than six strokes. He used to get upset hearing that shit but the game is the game. As long as he handles his business she won't ever have to think of way back when.

I haven't ran across a bitch myself that could pop pussy like that to make me bust like a volcano in record time.

Make me a believer that a couple of humps could give the kid the goose bumps. Then again, pussy can be a nigga's downfall. I don't wanna be fluffy like freshly whipped mashed potatoes. I *am* a thug.

I do believe one day though, that my idiotic thinking will catch up to me. Thugs need love too.

A Hoe's Danger

The streets are dangerous though. One of Blue's regular girls decided she would make some extra money doing her own thang outside of the familial structure that guaranteed her safety. Hard headed. Regardless, the girl thought she could save herself from having to give the house its cut of seventy- five dollars. While she was renegadin', she came across a trick she wasn't familiar with. This man was an out-of-towner.

No one ever knows for certain whether or not this man was in town on business or just passing through on some extra shit. Word was something creepy had been happening to working girls all over the Midwest. They were scandalously getting killed and found stankin' in hotel rooms, garbage receptacles, car trunks and alleyways. Some were sliced like deli meat and diced up like onions. Others had been found dismembered or beheaded. Some would be found burned to the bones, even still some weren't found at all. This murderer was a straight whore hater who deliberately set out to stalk working girls to torture and kill them.

The young girl went by the name Passionfruit. The stranger would pass her driving by a few times until she finally beckoned for him to meet her in a parking lot by the taco joint down on 23rd street. He gave her the name Jack when she asked him and claimed he was from Indiana. After the small talk he inquired about her services but didn't want to get down right away.

His mission was to gain her trust in order to eventually convince her to travel out of town with him. Acting out the role of a smooth criminally minded john, he had to impress upon the gal that he wasn't vice trying to arrest her for prostitution or solicitation.

A few days later he came back around looking for Passionfruit and when he found her asked her more personal questions. The girl didn't let all her business be known so she was leery of all the questions this mark was asking like: who did she work for, where' d she live, did she live alone, did she have any kids and what were her habits. Unbeknownst to Passionfruit, this man Jack had been secretly stalking her all along. He would sit in his van watching her daily from down the block with binoculars as she worked the strip over on Wisconsin Avenue. He would take notice to how many customers she pulled and ultimately came to the conclusion that she was going to be his next victim.

In his belief she had to perish because one, she was a prostitute. Two, she was beautiful. He believed beautiful women were dangerous. Three, she was black. Lastly, if she really had a loving family who gave a damn about her she wouldn't be out there everyday selling herself to survive.

To him there were no excuses or explanations that could justify such ignominious behavior.

Eventually, she became strangely familiar with Jack and turned him out in the parking lot by the taco joint that he noticed her going to four or five times a day. Jack would get a hard on just thinking of the ways he could hurt and cause her pain. He searched her out on a daily basis working up toward an eerie obsession that would ultimately bring the killer instinct out of him. He imagined himself being a tarantula sticking his fangs into a caterpillar injecting poison to make the poor insect succumb to a painful paralysis.

Since they've dated several times already, she began to let her guard down and started looking at him like a regular customer she could count on for a few extra hundred dollars a few times a week. After some dates they would go sit, have a bite to eat and talk about her dreams. If Jack had his way she wouldn't get the chance to make her dreams a reality.

Rule number one is never let your guard down no matter what the reasons. Friend or foe you never know who' s out to kill a hoe. Passionfruit had no idea that his game was all a plot to rid her of her existence on the planet. She had no clue that the man she spent time with was a cold-hearted blood drinker. Clues weren't available for pick up either. Always the perfect gentleman he never displayed any telltale signs of being a maniac. A clean-cut kind of guy with no habits except for his thirst for whore bloodshed was the only secret she wouldn't find out until later. Jack had invited her to take a trip with him to Chicago one weekend assuring her he would gladly pay her for her time spent with him. She was apprehensive but thinking of the money that she could get from him and the trip to the windy city quickly shut her anxieties down. She was expecting to cop a thousand dollars from him for the two-day weekend affair.

Passionfruit never saw that type of money coming from a trick unless she got slick and was able to pick his wallet.

On that Friday, he picked her up down the street from the house and she gave the excuse to Blue that she was going to spend some time with her family for the weekend and would return to work the upcoming Monday.

Ol' Jack took her out to eat at an inexpensive restaurant downtown and showed her some of the sights of Chicago. He never planned to drive back towards Milwaukee with her as the passenger but in order to get her to Chicago he had to tell her he would.

Passionfruit thought she was on top of world being shown around by a white man. A man willing to give her a thousand dollars to spend the weekend with him out of town.

She couldn't wait to tell the other girls the amount of money she had received just for kickin' it with someone in another town. She had already made plans for how she was going to spend the money, a nice portion of it going on a gift for Blue.

Meanwhile, he made plans to make her suffer for all her days of prostitution. Jack figured if she were ever unhappy about doing what she did for survival he would relieve her of those feelings. Permanently.

Returning to Milwaukee was not ever to be an option. For Jack had driven her to a remote part of the ghetto on Chicago's Westside near the projects with plans to bring her to her demise.

No one heard her stifling blood curdling screams and fucking with the Chi, if they did, they wouldn't have done shit to try to help her. Folks don't help each other cause they foresee the potential issue of having to deal with the pigs or unnecessary drama. Hell, the police could care less when a young black girl or woman for that matter gets killed. To them it's just another homicide to throw a cold case label on, oh well.

Passionfruit's mutilated body was found in a large green garbage receptacle behind an abandoned garage by some kids playing hide and seek in the ghetto. Her hands having been severed from her body, one was seen lying outside of the garbage can. Out of fright the oldest of the get-along gang opened the lid to the can to see an uncovered body. Running to tell some grownups about their discovery the boys were forever scarred by the sight they witnessed.

The carcass had been lacerated in ten different areas including her chest area where the nipples were sliced off exposing the tissues that made up the breast. Her thighs were gashed and inscribed with the design Star of David. Her two large toes had been chopped off and were found lodged in her anal cavity. Fingers had been broken backwards and some of her teeth were missing. A set of curling irons was left protruding from her vagina. When the authorities arrived to investigate the scene, they were astonished by the brutality of the crime. Forensics was able to determine the approximate time of death and together with federal agencies came to the conclusion that this latest victim was part of a series of unsolved murders throughout the Midwest.

As it turned out, Jack was being hunted for killing over eleven young black prostitutes in the Midwest for the past two years but his identity was never speculated. His profile was labeled after Jack the Ripper. No one ever saw him commit the crime so no one could come up with a possible description other than the fact that the perpetrator was more than likely a middle aged white man with enough money to travel and cruise the cities in search of victims.

Probably because he's a white man, he'll slide by with all of his murders. If he were a black or Hispanic man and the victims were white, he would have been hunted down like he was a member of the Taliban and burned at the stake for his heinous crimes. Everyone on the planet earth knows that the laws that were and are in effect didn't have good intentions for blacks when they were made anyway. The laws were made to work against us. We were guilty, until and if ever proven innocent.

When Monday had went and passed by Blue filed a missing person' s report on that following Wednesday worrying why she hadn't heard from the young girl. Deep down in the pit of her stomach and the core of her heart, Blue had a nagging premonition that something ugly had happened to the girl she named Passionfruit.

Normally when girls called themselves going against the grain, something or another usually happens to them. Oftentimes, the renegade had been kidnapped by some ruthless pimp and put out there in the streets to hoe from dusk to dawn. Other times the renegade has been killed by a trick. The law doesn't take those cases seriously.

News reports over the nation had chronicled the grisly murders and a five o' clock report caught Blue' s attention. Curiosity and concern led her to contact the news station broadcasting the latest, which in turn directed her to the proper authorities about her suspicions. Blue had been advised to make a trip to Chicago to try and identify the body found in the garbage can. She left for Chicago that early afternoon. Upon arriving at the city morgue she was led into a room where Passion' s body was being iced.

In hindsight, Blue recalled the girl telling her that she didn't have any immediate family in Milwaukee. In fact, LaTonya was a runaway from Tennessee. She got to Milwaukee by way of a pimp who called himself Hollywood. That nigga snatched her up from the bus station when he saw her at her most vulnerable; crying, neglected and lost. The combination of those factors is a pimp' s paradise. Hollywood introduced her to the hard knock life of the streets. He promised to take care of her every desire like getting her hair and nails done, buying her clothing, paying any bills she had including providing baby sitting services if she had any children. Hollywood also promised to show her the world through all the traveling they' d be doing together. Dawg ran the whole spill down to her. The only stipulation she would have had to get with was to become a concubine of sorts. Hearing that bullshit the way he said it, she was intrigued.

It didn't help the matter any more that Hollywood was a very good-looking light skinned brother with green eyes and naturally wavy hair. Girls catch the willies for men with those attributes when they don't know any better.

Remembering Tonya' s young pretty face and looking at the severely brutalized body threw Blue into a state of disbelief and shock. Never in her thirty plus years on this godforsaken earth has she ever seen anything as horrific as this. She's heard of the horror stories but had never seen it herself. Blue could only imagine the agony the young girl went through. Why didn't the girl call her with any information about who it was that she was with or a license plate number or something? She knew she was to check in at the least and let someone know she was alive and in one piece.

When no one knows anything about a trick and a girl decides to go off with him, she puts herself in grave danger especially if the trick is a natural born fool. Some of the crazy ones tend to be extremely charming and smooth with their game.

From that horrific incident forward, Blue made a carnal rule to the others that if she ever found out they were moonlighting on the side they could never work for her again. The price was too high to pay to have to deal with that.

The other girls didn't even need to hear that because once they heard what had happened to their fallen comrade, they didn't want that same thing to happen to them. The funeral was sad especially for the other gals because they didn't want to end up like Passionfruit.

In addition to her new rules, she also made admittance to the houses even stricter for the men to enter. She implemented the undertaking of doing background checks on the newer clients and photocopying identification, all for safety precautions.

Deep down inside, Blue felt that that murder wasn't going to be the last from the stranger who cold bloodily murdered Passionfruit. As of yet, there was nothing that could be done to find him and make him suffer for his murders. So far all of his executions had been carried out flawlessly.

Killa

After that latest murder, Jack decided to lay low in Milwaukee for a few months. Renting a room at an extended stay motel it was as if he was on a sabbatical leave to study his next plans for slaughter. Since no one knew what he looked like he was free to roam around and case out more girls.

His strange preference for only black girls was sickening especially since he came across many white whores in traffic. Investigators were busy trying to understand how it was that this serial killer didn't make girls from other ethnicities victims.

Jack was highly systematic in the manner of which he stalked his sheep. Capable of strategically planning who he was going to kill and where the murder would take place it could take him as long as several weeks to get it down to the most minute detail.

His obsession with sex only urged him on. The thoughts of soft then brute sex with a black woman was like a flaming crippling desire that had to be extinguished only with her losing her life of course.

An earlier victim of Jack' s happened to be a twenty-something flawlessly natural looking sophomore who went to school in Michigan at the state university named Alexis. What attracted him to her was her display of self-confidence and assurance about the way she strutted around in her six-inch heels in the strip club. She pranced like she owned and controlled everything in the club from the bouncers to the stage to the bar. Everywhere she waltzed heads turned men and women alike. She knew she was hot to trot. Sending off vibes that she was unattainable only made his not quite six inch dick harder.

Alexis had the body of a trained dancer. Long muscular toned legs, a high protruding ass that was perfectly round in shape, a small waist and perky breasts equal in size to small nectarines. It was easy to witness how she made a lot of money in the club. Her deep brown complexion only made her more compelling. More deadly in a sense.

His game plan was to ask her to perform for him in the champagne room. Once he was able to secure themselves from roaming eyes he enticed her with even more money than the two hundred he already had to give her to get up there. Money wasn't an issue for him.

After an hour in the champagne room and five hundred dollars spent, plans had been made to hook up later in the week for a private lunch engagement and late afternoon drive to the country.

That lunch that day was Alexis' s last meal. Her body had been found mangled in a cornfield by a farmer tending his land.

Charm was Jack' s motto. Money was his booby trap. Murder was his niche.

Family Issues

Back at the ranch, my mother fell ill so I made it my business to stay in close proximity to ensure her well-being was intact. After visiting the doctor with her, I received the bad news that my beautiful mother was dying slowly and from the disease called cancer. The doctor said it hadn't reached full-blown status yet but it would be wise of me to begin preparation. It's a good thing five years ago that she purchased a life insurance policy worth over $500,000.

I never thought what life would be like without my mother. She's everything to me, my guidance, friend, teacher, and love of my life. From now on I'm going to make a more conscious effort to spend more time with her.

Nowadays kids don't really know their parents, too busy ripping and running in the streets. Since my biological father wasn't anywhere to be found she was woman enough to take on both responsibilities. My mother could have given up on me and pursued her dreams without me but she stayed. She could have aborted me but she didn' t. And for that, I am going to reward her with my time, patience and devotion. Phyllis deserves that and then some. I'm in love with her. She's the only woman who can make me sit down and listen or tell me how high to jump and I would leap like a frog.

I can remember the days of when we would go to the grocery store and see other mothers fall short by a few dollars or foodstamps. I would be embarrassed for the not haves from all the stares and the clearing of the throats, but mom would always help them out. A true playa.

When some of her friends lights were cut off cuz they didn't have the change to pay the bill and had to use candles, mom would look out. I remember the days of when some neighbor' s gas was cut off and they had to eat cold cuts and bathe in cold water. She paid the tax on their bill cuz of the kids. Playerism at its best.

Now those days weren't too bad when it was hot as hell outside. I can even remember when I needed new gear to wear and she would go sweat a store for their shit, coming home with bags of clothes with sensor tags still on them. Hell, I can remember when the car would break down and moms would have to use her womanly charms to get the car fixed on a discount or for free.

Yea, those are the old ass days. Some good and some bad, but my momma was no joke.

As a man I can understand that women sometimes have to do things out of character in order to solidify some stability and make ends meet. Whether its going to clothing stores and boosting some gear or walking in the grocery store and walking out with purses full of meat, deodorant, toothpaste or whatever. Women will garner that iron will to put their ass on the market to make ends meet. That's why when all else fails pussy will always sell.

Exasperation With Elevation

Ughh!! I swear men can really get on my last fuckin' nerves! One minute they behave and the next minute they need to be enrolled in training classes just like the dogs they are. They act like puppies at first all full of love and playfulness then they mature to mutt status. The assholes get lazy and cheap but stay horny. Then they have the gotdamn nerves to think that they can just lay up in the pussy and prop their feet up on the furniture like everything's all cool and shit.

When I have to show them differently the next move they play is to cop an attitude and proclaim I'm the one on the trip tip. Yea I'm tripping. Like I should be happy because they around keeping me company. Hell I can keep myself company. I tell them all the time I can buy a dick to suck and fuck whenever necessary and even some of the dicks are operable by batteries.

Niggas betta recognize the true in me and respect my gangsta.

These fake ass Romeos get on my damn nerves too. Hollerin' at me about what they have and what they can do for me if I just give in and cooperate. Straight frontin' is all they are good for. Their game is as transparent as an empty glass full of water. Catch my drift? See, one minute their full of empty promises and will tell me anything to make me end up telling my girls that "Girl, he told me he like my spirit," type shit. And I know better than that because the main thing on any niggas mind is how he's gonna

49

try to stick his dick in me and force me to holla out his name like he king dingaling or something.

Then there' s the balla type of stud who thinks that every single woman is enthralled with him sportin' one carat total weight diamond earrings, a bezel, Rolex watches and rollin' a Q45 or Lexus. That shit is cool and all but really impress a bitch like me by lacing me with a lady' s Rolex and buying me a slick ride. Better yet, buy me a house.

If a man can do that then he's a cold muthafucka. A lot of these hoes get starstruck and ultimately end up losing themselves for absolutely nothing to gain. Men with money are like that. They know a lot of hoes are desperate and willing to give up the ass quick as lightning so they play on the girl's mental and before you know it …it's a wrap. Chickenheads flock to the rooster and the rooster loves to fuck with all the chickenheads, as many as possible. Yuck! Nasty ass niggas.

For some strange reason I can't seem to be able to find a good man, maintain the relationship and live happily. Instead, I always find myself involved with men who love to cheat, misuse and neglect. That's why I have the "fuck a man" attitude because they all need colonoscopies.

Even married men are full of shit. They make vows before God and still act foolish anyway. Where are the real men? And I don't even want the ones who are on the prowl on the down low either. Why on earth would I want to kiss on a man who' s been sucking on another man' s dick and licking assholes? These days are ill.

In the end I know that I'm my own best friend. I've been hurt and survived. Every one of those times I've been hurt I learned a lot about myself in the process. I learned that I'm much stronger than what they think and I push on. I used to daydream about being with a particular person in a certain way having kids and shit. I fell for a lot of garbage but time helped me move on from the crying and all the disappointment. There have been times when my own buddies would warn me about messing with certain characters but me being the person that I am, have the tendency to give people the benefit of the doubt and low and behold …t hey always fail me.

Eventually, they always seem to try and come around after they've been through some life changing shit. But by then, it's way too late. "Oh, I don't want your sorry ass now," I tell them. Shoulda been right the first time. Leave the trickery and games to the chirren. I'm a grown ass woman.

For once it would be nice to meet someone and hit it off and the four dots actually connect. I know I'm not the only one in this world that would love to meet that super special someone. I can't be. Am I wrong for being tired of all the hazardous men? Bullshit pours down like rain that's why I have a Teflon umbrella.

Some people have the nerve to chastise me for being attracted to women. Maybe a woman would treat me like I deserve to be treated, with respect and some loyalty. Yea, I've had my flings with a few women here and there. I'm not sure if I'm bisexual or not cuz I don't have the desire to put my mouth on a woman but

I'll definitely let a woman get down on me. I've had pretty bitches fuck me. They are nice to wake up to. The ugly chicks were able to get a shot of ass too. I didn't discriminate. But for them, I had to be straight up horny as hell.

Like this one chick named Fifi. She was pretty hard on the vision but the bitch could dine the shit outta some pussy. She knew to be gentle on the pearl plus she knew how to execute a deep deliberate finger fuckin'. A pretty one like Michelle who looked like a video hoe was absolutely gorgeous. She was Creole with hair that came down to her ass with a cute shape, nice tits, plump ass, pretty face and definitely with a personality all of her own. Definitely a rare find. As far as her skills between the sheets, she was rough on the clit and my shit is sensitive. But hey, she was pretty as hell.

I experienced the feeling that a man does when it's a lovely thing to gaze down at a pretty woman performing oral sex on him. Looking down at Michelle was like whoa.

Fuckin' with women isn't where my heart is but a girl gotta do what a girl gotta do. And on that note, I better come up with a game plan to get this new furniture I want for my living room. Shiid, a bitch just may have to make a move out of town for a week. Perhaps I'll go up north somewhere to work at one of those white clubs. The Italian leather sectional pieces I want cost about four thousand alone. I figure if I can hustle up at half of that I'll be cool. Yea, I'll sell some twat here and there for the right price. Hopefully, I'll be able to catch at least six quick dates for three hundred and the rest can come from tips. I have to set a quota to get my mind right for the grind. I strip every now and then to supplement my agenda.

Oh boy, its time for me to evaluate and reflect on my own shit with praises of course. Sometimes we sisters have to do that to maintain our sanity and keep our dignity in check.

Let's see, I'm twenty-three year old. Shit, I don't have any children yet thank goodness. Not that I have something against the little crumb-snatchers, its just that I'm not emotionally ready and financially stable to take care of any like I would care too. I know way to many young women with babies that are struggling to survive and make ends meet. Hustlin' working two jobs at a time to stripping their clothes off and prostituting to make amends. I ain't mad at them the babies gotta eat.

The fathers are usually deadbeat bustas trying to be Casanovas with all their half slickness. Besides, the job of being both a father and a mother doesn't appeal too much to me at all. I like to get up and go whenever I feel like it anyway and I take great pride in being careful.

I have a high school diploma and a college education under my belt. School was always stressed in my family as the most important attribute a young black person could ever have in this world besides a pocket full of money. I'm grateful to have a decent ride and a place to call my own as long as the damn rent is paid on time. With all of that to boot, I still find it hard to sustain a comfortable relationship with a man whose trying to have thangs in this lifetime. Rims, clothes and hoes is the mantra nowadays for these fools. Forget about the real shit like companionship, loyalty and true love.

Oh well, from now on I'm going to put my energies into concentrating on me and my goals which is the best thing for me to do anyhow. When that time comes for me to get with a real true to life man I'll recognize him but he gotta come correct. Bullshitters need not to come at all.

Most dudes are ok but half of them are not. A lot of niggas just ain't for the right thang. Guys have the nerve to be picky when they runnin' around with five and six babies with at least four different baby mommas. Don't let me forget about the type of man that will steal from you. I've been in that situation too. The nigga was jealous because I'm able to handle my business far better than what he's ever able to. It was always my belief that a woman and man were supposed to be down for each other having each other's back. Boy, didn't I learn differently. Well it was like that in one of my relationships. Yea, I've slept with the enemy. Damn near been killed by the enemy but I'm a survivor. Nah, that ain't the right word. I am a warrior. That's why I have the attitude I have now. A lot of peeps think I'm psycho.

Like my girl Lynn Whitfield in that movie A Thin Line Between Love and Hate, leave me the hell alone if your intentions aren't good and real because once I let you in and you fuck me over ...I ' ll become hostile.

A lot of jerks get happy as hell to run into a broad like me without kids. They think they won't have any responsibilities in dealing with me. Little do they know I'm a huge responsibility. Again, no just layin' up in the ass ' round here pardna, nigga go outside in the garage, grab the rake and take care of my lawn. A weak muthafucka gotta bow down. I need a man that knows what to do; I'm tired of training these mutts.

It seems to me that all the good guys have the bad girls and the bad guys have the good girls. Hell, when will a good girl be able to hook up with a good guy and they both can be bad together? That's what I want in my life, a man that wants to be down for the cause. Me. A lot of them are undercover bitches and cowards. Always talking' bout what they wanna do and their lives ain't worth the piss that leaks from their penises and stains their drawers.

So it's for me to stay on the grind and make shit happen for myself cuz if I don' t, who will? Determination is a muthafucka and I need a man to be on my level. I'm a purebred way serious bout my bank and life.

Friends? I don't have many girlfriends because they're plastic. I had broads in my life that I thought were cool and down with me but in reality deep down they were against me. They were jealous of my abilities to flip script and maintain confidence in any given situation. The hoes were mad at me because I was myself being that I didn't fit the normal everyday stigma of the so-called modern day bitch. Fuck a stigma! I get off on the beat of my own drum-no time to be ashamed. What kind of person has the nerve to perpetrate the fraud actin' like a friend when they turn around and steal from you? A fucking ingrate!

My melody is catastrophic in the sense that attempting to groove to my shit being phony will only bring forth disaster, dismay, and an ugly ass tune. The only plastic I need in my life is the kind that preserves my food and the kind that' ll get me shit I can pay for on a later date.

Shit, I haven't even told you my name. It's Jane't, that's pronounced with the t being silent; it sort of has a French twang to it. I come from a two-parent household and I also have two brothers. One brother, the oldest is full blooded and my other older brother I gained from my father. Yea, Pops was a rollin' stone.

My parents were married for over fifteen years. Growing up, I can't really say my household was the leave it to Leroy kind of home but it was functional. My mother and father are originally from the south and they migrated up north back in the seventies for the chance at a better life.

Both of my parents graduated from high school and were able to land factory jobs here in Milwaukee at the top factory in town. From the beginning my parents didn't want to send my sibling and myself to public education schools. Therefore, they slaved and worked extra long hours on the job in order to pay for private schooling. Tuition at one of those schools would easily run them a couple of thousand dollars a semester. Nowadays folks can fill out for a voucher and get in where they fit in. That just ain't fair to my parents who had to slave and do without to pay the tuition for us to go to school.

My brother Pat would only be able to attend school for a short while, until he got either suspended or kicked out for being a mishap or class clown. To this day I still don't understand what made him waste our parents hard-earned money. That bread could have been put to good use like investments perhaps. Once he was kicked out of the privileged school, he would be shipped around from one school to the next. Boy did that anger Daddy and stress Mom.

Pat was always in trouble for one thing or the other. And my parents just couldn't quite figure out what to do with him. Continuous punishments and whippings didn't do the trick either. He would still act a plum fool knowing fully well they would get pissed and would want to crack his skull down to the white meat. I don't know if he was acting out and was craving attention or whether or not he suffered from mental problems that should have been addressed by a professional. Either way, I don't think my brother had it all upstairs. Maybe the doctor accidentally dropped him after his delivery. I always used to hear of shit like that happening.

I, on the other hand, was the baby in the family. Since I was a little girl, our parents believed they wouldn't have any trouble rearing me. Beliefs can be untrue sometimes. Also, I was a Daddy's girl. Anyone who knows anything about two parent families knows that the boys are Momma's boys and the girls are Daddy's girls.

I don't really remember my father and I spending a lot of time together when I was a child maybe because he was always at work. The nickname my father gave me that lasted throughout my adulthood was the moniker Cat.

Yep, I was dear Daddy' s pussycat. Whenever he would see me coming he' d be like, "Hey Cat!" Man, I miss those days.

Kids just don't realize how good they have it when small and dependent on parents who actually are good parents. At least while they're young they don't have to worry about the electric or gas bill, rent, gas for the car if they're not on the bus, food, clothes or anything else. All of that sneaks up on us once we leave the safety nest.

Believe me, I took my dear sweet time breaking away too. My oldest brother Pat on the flip side, had to learn about life early starting when he was about fifteen. He ended up getting in trouble with the law on many different levels. I suppose he was hustling to make a dollar or two.

Anyhow that's a glimpse into my childhood life. I was fortunate enough to grow up in a two-parent home. Everything wasn't all peaches and cream but at that time, we were a family. As the years passed, the drugs of the streets infiltrated my once strongly knit family. With that, the family began to disintegrate slowly but surely.

I know for a fact that every single family in the United States has one or a few family members that fall victim to drugs. My advice to those experiencing it is this: watch your shit with eagle eyes or else you' ll end up missing something. How do I know? Easy. I lost plenty of shit at the hands of a drug addict that was once considered trustworthy. My educated guess is drugs will rule the streets until the nonexistence of man whether the drugs are prescribed or not.

Now back to me personally. I was a goody two shoes until my early twenties. I had a boyfriend who had hustlers in his family and I mean that with capitol letters. Anywho, I paid attention to how they were living lavishly for free. I wanted some dibs in that too. Why should I bust my ass at a nine to five to spend my hard earned money when I can deal with them and get my shit plus a whole lot more at a great five finger discount?

I learned how to boost clothes and definitely not the cheap shit. I'm talking about boutique clothing like Cache, La Pearlz, Aversa, Vertigo and Bourgeoise. Other mainstream gear like Donna Karan, DKNY, Gucci, Prada, and Bebe were standard wear for me. Why have I broken off stores like that? It's simple. Because the shit was far too highly priced for what I cared to spend my hard earned money on. Hell, I even have a few Armani pieces in my collection of fine wear. But some gear I wouldn't pilfer would be that Gigi Hunter line. She's a sista, so I just couldn't do that. Purses and shoes were on the hit list as well. While hoes stunt in the fake Coach, Fendi and Louis Vuitton purses I choose to rock an authentic Ferragamo or Marc Jacobs. Currently, I'm working on copping a Mischka crocodile bag with the sling back high heels to match. Gotta have the accessories with the fits or it' d be a fashion faux.

Eventually, I had to upgrade my hustle to turning out my flat into Taj Mahal. I have mad furniture from Eddie Bauer, Pottery Barn, Pier 1, Ethan Allen and Sears Homelife. Plus, in my living and bedroom are four thousand dollar grandfather clocks. I was never the type to go out and get forty-five pieces of furniture for eight hundred dollars. I've been to folks house and I swear all I see is the cheap panther rug, statues and gold painted stands. Then for the bedroom sets, I've seen that cheap black laminated trimmed in fake gold shit with the matching chest and dresser. The lamps included in the forty-five-piece package deal looked like lamps that came from a resale shop.

Folks actually think they doin' the damn thang. I can spot cheap shit with my eyes half shut. Lemme stop, cuz that's maybe all they can afford. Hell, my living room drapes alone cost more than twelve hundred. Velvet, silk and chiffon grace my windows. I don't play.

I was never into having blinds hanging from my windows but if the blinds were made of leather then I'd definitely have to cop that with some custom made leather and suede furniture to set it off.

I'm liable to walk in a store without a bag and walk out with a three thousand dollar refrigerator on wheels. What? I love beautiful things and if I want it, it's for me to get it. How simple is that? By any means necessary. The hustle is beneficial.

Some may consider me to be materialistic and that's ok. I just love to surround myself with nice quality things. My mouth salivates for quality anything less is uncivilized. Maybe one day I'll get up with a top-notch nigga that can and will equal my drive and tastes.

Pray for ya' girl. Sheesh, its rough swimming out here in this sea of sharks.

Sweatin'

I had been hustling like a crazed madman and I promised Mom that before everything was all said and done that I would buy her a special house designed by me and I did just that. Though I have to admit, if it weren't for Blue I would have had a much harder time in accomplishing my goals. It's cool to have plugs in different areas.

Once I had saved up ten thousand I went to Blue with a plan. I knew she would help my cause and to me, that was all good. The house was incredibly shabby and in a rundown part of town but I knew I could funk it out. I was lucky to cop it too. The city only wanted seven thousand for it, Blue was able to get it for me for sixty-four hundred. With the money left over I invested it into the paints needed, flooring, bathroom fixtures and carpeting. I knew drug addicts that were skilled in the plumbing and electricity fields. That part didn't run me in the hole too much cuz for a little bit of dope, the work can get done professionally. Imagine that.

The house was located on twenty-fifth and Vine. The neighborhood was well known for having drug spots all around the place. However, gentrification was currently taking place and the city was shutting down those spots, condemning them or selling them at dirt-cheap prices. The house I bought was a duplex so it had double everything and the basement was large. After the plumbing and electrical issues were dealt with I hired more people to do the painting. I began with the upper portion of the house. In the kitchen I had the walls painted a very pale yellow and the ceiling was stuccoed. The floors were yellow swirl marble tiled. Once that was completed the kitchen sink and cabinets were specially custom ordered. The appliances were going to be bought by this white girl, Kelly. She hustles with credit cards and checks so I needed her in my life for a little while. The stove and refrigerator I had in mind were the stainless steel sets that come with the dishwasher and microwave. The island had to be specially ordered. Kelly plugged me with all that shit for half of what it cost.

The bathroom upstairs was small but on the other side of it was a closet that had to be demolished. With the space being more open the bathroom was large enough to fit a custom made cream empress finished bathtub with jets into the space while having plenty of room left over to add more customized bathroom finishing. I decided to make the floors of this washroom white marble with the walls painted a light cream color. Many different decorations could be utilized with that color scheme. The new sink, toilet and bidet were cream colored also. To me, the bathroom had a Spanish feel to it for the walls were stuccoed. An Egyptian tiled chaise was placed against the wall and now the bathroom had two doors with one leading into a bedroom.

Now of course the bedrooms would have to be slammin' and since there were three upstairs and connected, once again I had a wall knocked out to enlarge the master suite.

That way a California king sized bed would fit along with the other amenities. Built in shelves had to be put in for space. Those walls were painted a light mauve with matching plush, fall when you step on it type carpeting. Damn, I should become an interior decorator. My skills would net me royal pay. I bought a six thousand dollar chandelier to replace the paltry light fixture and installed a vanity for mother.

The guestroom would contain a trundle daybed from Pottery Barn, a desk hutch and chair plus a few bookshelves for a library.

The dining room floors were refinished and the walls were painted a very light red, the woodwork in the house was exceptionally installed in pine and oak. Lastly, the living room was painted an eggshell color with plush cream carpeting and a mantelpiece was added to give the room a cozier feel to it.

Once completed the upstairs was pimpish. I knew mom would love it! Her little man was a man of style, taste and flavor. Kelly would help me furnish the place for half price or for some dick. The latter would have to do now that I think about it. All of the decorating upstairs took about a month and a half.

The crackheads were putting in overtime. Rockstars need some credit for their skills yet and still I need to make sure I get a state of the art burglary alarm system installed. Just for safety measures of course. I wasn't too much in a rush for the downstairs although I wanted to put a spiral staircase stemming from the upstairs living room to the downstairs living room.

When I do get finished with the entire house that once cost sixty-four hundred, it would be worth ten times that. As long as the hustle keeps going strong I can have the downstairs completed shortly, have new siding and stone put on the outside plus have a lighted gated fence put around the house. It's all good in the hood. Kelly really came through for me when I needed her. I met her at the mall. Now dig, I ain't too much into them like that but this was one fine ass snow bunny. Built like the original Mothers of the Earth but lacking the melanin, she stood like a stallion.

She's the type of broad that could walk into any store and handle major business without ever being questioned once. I like her too. She's not the type of snow bunny that tries too hard to be down, in fact, she doesn't exhibit any of the mannerisms. There's nothing worse than a white person trying to act black. Hoes like that turn me off with the little ethnic inspired hairdo's, baggy clothes, strange soundin' curse words and neck swiveling shit. Hell, be yourself. I knew I could come up with her easy, the rhythm towards me was loud and clear like the sounds of a rock concert.

We were in a department store at one of the upscale malls in town, and I was looking for an outfit to wear to the club. She was in the adjoining section of the men's section and I peeped her spying on a playa. So after our eyes locked a few times I beckoned for her to step into my realm. Her curiosity got the best of her and she took the bait. After our introductions we chatted for a short while she asked what it was that I was looking for. I let her pick me out an outfit and the broad bought it for me. She had the nerve to try and check shit in letting me know that I was to wear the gear when I took her out for dinner later that night.

Hmmm, being aggressive and assertive are two fine qualities a pretty woman can have. I don't like those rollover broads unless they're bringing me some damn money. A lot of niggas I know love to hook up with those spineless, weak ass women. Fuck that! Give me a woman that can hold it down when shit gets crazy. After I left her in the mall, I went to get a shave and haircut. A brother gotta be looking fly, especially when sportin' a quarter piece on his arm. I wonder what she'll look like later. She was very classy looking today, so this oughta interesting. I may take her to the Italian restaurant on Jackson Street for dinner then maybe to a little bar further down the street. I thought to myself that I could end up liking her a great deal.

I found out later in our early relationship that Kelly was a trust fund baby. Being a trust fund baby is practically unheard of in black families. Shit, we are born either in poverty or if you're lucky, born into the middle class but hardly ever of a trust fund manner. Even though I heard all the stories I can't still fully understand why a lot of us were always at the bottom of the totem pole. According to law other ethnicities get to come to America on a pass and set up shop for free having the nerve to think that we are lazy.

Kelly was a tall beauty with a nice ass for a white broad, green- eyed, possessing a dazzling Colgate smile. Her wheat colored hair was straight with hot blond streaks, very lovely looking. Anyhow, her parents didn't send her to public schools but to high priced academies for girls. She had expressed to me that she didn't really see her parents a lot while growing up; basically the schools and nannies raised her.

For the life of me, I don't understand why she chose to live the life of a criminal. When I inquired about it her reply was simple, doing things your not supposed to do adds spice to an otherwise morbidly boring secure life like hers. Besides she knew she could get away with it because of her looks alone. If black women had it easy like that this world would definitely be a better place.

I had also asked her about her obvious attraction to black men. After a long discussion of how her parents were from the old south and that her great granddad was a prominent member of the Klan, it was easier for her to want the forbidden fruit. They would be highly upset knowing that their precious babygirl was bound to get dicked down by a mandingo. Too gotdamn bad, her spit shall be on this dick. White people are a trip.

As terrible as it may seem, the only way blacks come up in this fucked up world is either thru entertainment, sports, or hustling but as a trust fund baby? Hardly. Should I have mixed feelings? Nah, she'll serve her purpose in my life to the fullest. I won't be an experiment for her fantasies of getting dicked down by a black man without being paid in full. Call me a cut throat nigga if you wanna. I'll take that charge. I can't fathom the thought of being anything other than hustler.

Kelly lived on the downtown east side of Milwaukee near the lake. The rents in that area range from eight hundred to thirteen hundred monthly depending on the layout. She drove a 600SLE and had a small terrier pup. Her apartment was modernly decorated with expensive modern Italian furnishings and classic black art. Interesting.

My main plan is to get what I can from her while still being nice. I'd hate for her gramps to put his klan mob on me. Who the hell am I kidding, this ain't the old south, muthafuckas do have the equal opportunity of catchin' buckshots.

I picked her up from her place in my whip ' round six o' clock. Her style was refreshingly crisp- a black knit dress that clung to her ample cleavage and she was wearing some fly ass shoes. The heels on her feet were so dope I had to ask her what kind of shoes they were and her reply was Jimmy Choos. Ah, I've heard of a few rapper bitches spittin' about those. Anyhow she was well put together. Her hair looked like it' d been roller set and cascaded down her shoulders. With hardly any jewelry on, she could have passed for a model easily or a well paid hooker. She made that implant assed singer look like nothing. I'm sure that came from the nanny' s milk her grandmother sucked and it skipped a coupla' generations reaching her. One black drop is all you need.

Together we both looked like money. Hers from old money, mine came from hard labor hustling.

As we sat in Elsa' s on the avenue, we sipped Dom Perignon champagne, ordered filet of mignon and the strawberry concocted dessert. The majority of the white men inside were from corporate America, were in awe of her beauty and I even recognized some of them as users. A couple of ballas I knew were in the area where we were eating and scooping Kelly out.

I felt great having a lovely dinner, money in my pocket and a beautiful woman at my side. Not to shit on the sistas but I know damn well I ain't the only black person in this world that trips on seeing niggas with ugly out of shape white bitches. At least mine is top notch.

I was on top of the world and the evening just begun. After supper we headed down the street to this small intimate bar for a few martinis. There weren't many people inside yet so we had time to relax and enjoy ourselves before the crowd came gallopin' in.

To end our evening, we went for a walk and enjoyed the dance of the stars. Kelly wanted me to come over to her place for a nightcap but I didn't want to push things any quicker than necessary. If this girl isn't careful she could fall in love with a playa. I'm not ready for a full-fledged relationship for I still had a lot of hustling and pimpin' of the streets to do before I settle down. The streets are my life, the streets made me who I am today with the help of my mother. The streets may be where I'll eventually meet my maker. Right now, I belong to the streets. So all that mushy shit gotta take the backseat.

I walked Kelly to her apartment door and bent down to kiss her forehead goodnight but she tilted her head upward kissing me square on the mouth. Damn, she didn't even have the usual white folks stale cheese eater breath either. That shit be all stank. That stolen kiss is gonna cost her. Her lips were all soft and shit, but for the sake of brotherhood and my ancestors, I had to be strong. I stopped kissing a long ass time ago. I'mma playa. She gots to pay me before I slang this dick her way. Dang, I sound like one of *those* kinds of bitches. When the time is right, I'll fuck the dog shit out of her, knock the bottom out but not tonight, not yet. She looked sad when I turned to walk away and there saw a look of longing in her eyes. Kelly looked vulnerable like a hungry lost kitten. Hungrily in heat for some dick I bet. Soon enough I'll make her purr but I need to get in the streets and get on my grind.

The streets made me. I'm constantly in them every day of the muthafuckin' year. Leap year included.

Back in da hood, I ran into Loc and he had some work for me to do. That work could net me four stacks. I had to drop off a package to his peoples down on Cherry Street and bring back some money. So I went and put my Cadillac up and switched into my old trusty hooptie, Lilly. I love that car, it didn't bring me any unwanted attention and I could make this trip without the hassles of dealing with the crooked ass pigs that catered to upholding the law only when it suited them best. I'll holla on that later though. When Loc handed me the package, I secured it into the vacuum cleaner I had in the trunk and put it in the backseat of my ride.

After this run I'm going to stop off at the strip club, Stargazers, and see who' s shaking tonight. I could go for listening to some rap and looking at the young hoes that like to fuck nigga's faces and get paid. I ain't mad at them. With all respects, I can give props to the big assed girls with cute faces gettin' at they change. A certain kind of strength is necessary for a woman to put up with the shit in the tittie clubs that we men tend to give them.

Truthfully, I like a woman that gets down for hers. I heard from an old head that it ain't trickin' if you got it. I might pay for some skullduggery. The bitch gotta have a pretty face and she definitely gotta know how to work the ass muscles. Hmmm, I'll take two fifties and a couple twenties for that purpose alone. I just might pay for two bitches to slurp on me. What the hell? One can bob on these balls and the other can handle the brain.

The drop off transaction went smooth and those niggas down on Cherry were gamblin' in the trap. I almost got in on a game but I had plans to go to the club tonight. Business was handled, now it was time to party.

I put away thirty-five hundred of the money and kept the remaining five to trick off. I had to change from my sweat clothes into this black FUBU jean and leather outfit. I tossed the K-Swiss tennis shoes for a pair of Birdmans. I put my three-carat diamond earrings in my ears, put on my Jacob watch, platinum chain, crunched out medallion, six-carat diamond pinky ring and dabbed my neck with some African body oil. To look at me you could only say, "now thas a Playa for real." I went out to the garage to pull the ' Lac back out into the limelight. The hoes are gonna love me or love me not.

The club I was headed to was located uptown on Fond du Lac Avenue and there was another club less than fifteen minutes away from the one I was going to. I may stop off at both spots before the night is over to pop a bottle or two.

As I pulled into the parking lot I noticed a lot of my niggas cars were parked there too. The line to Stargazers had at least twenty people waiting to get in and as usual I noticed many different women waiting to get inside. The ladies were looking nice and I didn't want any of them. Not even the pussy. I know their type. Have kids at home sleeping, no jobs, and no cars. They carpool and then the little change they did come across was spent on getting their nails, hair, and outfits in order.

No thanks, I like the type of woman who doesn't try so hard. I mean these hoes come out every day of the week dressed in the seven dollar per outfit clothes sportin' cheap Faker shoes. Some of the hard ass hairstyles they be wearing is late. That shit be looking like a tub of black gel was used to make it mold. I can only imagine how many containers of shampoo are needed to wash that gunk out. Men can tell who tries too hard to look good and who's natural with the flavor.

The club was not yet packed so I was able to grab a drink with simplicity, come up on a seat near the back wall to watch all the happenings. The DJ was spinning the sounds of some old school rap. In fact, he was spinning some Eric B. and Rakim, I couldn't help but to bob my head to "Paid In Full" when I suddenly checked this chick eyeballin' me up and down. On the real, I felt like a piece of meat. I wonder is this how women feel when I gawk at them. I don't know who she was or who she thought I was but she came over saying, "what up." What the hell kind of bullshit is that? Not a muthafuckin' thang over here, then this broad got even more bold and said to me, "Let's go to the hotel tonight."

Oh yea? I'll pass on that, I ain't puttin' nothing past a hoe. She peeped all this ice and wanna roll out with me. Fast pussy is skeptical to me and I certainly don't want it from a bitch with saggy ass titties, a face plastered with makeup, a seriously unnatural kitchen weave and two capped gold teeth on the front of her grill.

When I didn't reply, she started dancing all up on me, like putting her ass to my dick was supposed to turn me on. I sidestepped her desperate ass and the hoe had the nerve to follow me around the club piranha style. Now don't get it twisted, the hoe wasn't super dog ugly or nothing but I know she was only at me because of my gear and jewelry. Star struck ass buzzard.

Most chickenheads act like that, thinking how a nigga's dressed tells how much bread he's holding. I know many a broke nigga that got a wardrobe to flex hard in and pockets full of lint. I had to tell the hoe to back off cuz I was married. She backed off all right but continued to eagle eye me throughout the night. She trying just a little too damn hard, for all I know some nigga probably sic' n her on me for the set up.

While I was walking around the club upstairs I didn't see much so I descended down the stairs and midway I stopped to formulate my next move. I was standing behind some girl and her ass looked lovingly juicy in them jeans. She wasn't all dressed up or nothing.

Actually she was just chillin' in some jeans and a top. When she turned around, that's when I remembered her. I knew this chick from another bar down on Locust Street called Tap One and she was cool peoples. I was always glad to see her, a very nice girl who I never saw drinkin, smoking or hanging with a lot of buzzards. I can't remember her name but I never forgot the cute face. After she turned around she noticed me too and we immediately hugged.

This little black girl doesn't know that I always liked her attitude and smile. I haven't seen her for a long while and it was *definitely* nice to see her again. I had to ask her name again and she told me that it was Jane't. Ah, I remember now. We took our conversation downstairs and I asked if I could take her to breakfast some time. We exchanged numbers and hugged again. I swear from huggin' on her I felt a jolt of energy shoot through my body similar to electrocution. That's some powerful shit. I'll take that charge.

Throughout the rest of the night I kept my eyes on her to peep who else was diggin' her. Needless to say, a lot of muthafuckas showed her plenty of love. She's definitely someone I want to get to know better. Niggas in the streets have always talked up on her. She was a change from the ordinary rats, a sweet girl. I remember when she used to come in the club Tap One. It was like the music stopped upon her arrival. Everybody took notice of her. Killer part is, its not like she was doing anything extraordinary to get the attention she unknowingly commanded.

However, me being a boss playa and all, I would have to allow her to call me first. It' d be a shame for me to appear as if, *I,m* sweatin' her. Nope, can't do that one, I do have a rep to maintain. I'm the man, gotta keep the upper hand.

I'm glad I came to the club tonight. Ol' eagle eyes was slicing me with her gaze. Somethin' s strange about that one. She's at me just a little too hard. I know I look good and all but gotdamn.

When my night was over I went to the crib and hoped Jane't would call but when she didn't I figured she would call later on tomorrow. We could set up a date for a night on the town. I wanna get up with her alright. I know when I lay this pipe in her ass, she'll be hooked on a nigga. On second thought, I would make love to her to her delicate ass.

No Need To Floss- I Got This

It has been a mighty long time since I went out and actually had a good time, but I just had to go the other night. Being a homebody was normal activity for me especially since I got the Internet. I swear I love meeting people from all over the world and chatting with them, exchanging e-mails and playing computer games on Yahoo when my punk ass internet provider isn't constantly booting me off for one reason or another. Those muthafuckas got the nerve to charge me twenty-three dollars and ninety cents a month for their bullshit. I got a plan for they asses though.

The Internet probably stopped a lot of people from running the streets and getting into trouble. But I was becoming a little too dependent on that computer so I went to the mall looking for a shirt or something to wear out. Since I didn't see anything too much that I wanted I just settled for my trusty blue jeans and a top I had boosted from Chicago.

I hustled like that every now and then. I learned how from a set of one of my ex' s nieces. Those twins were cold at the store game. They would saunter into a store empty handed and in like five minutes would roll damn near a whole rack of clothes into a garbage bag and swagger out the store like ain't shit happened. In a couple of hours they would have over five thousand dollars worth of merchandise easily. Everythang and anythang was subject to get heisted if they had anything to do with it. Clothes; shoes; purses;

make-up; coats; underwear; house wares; gasoline; medicine and food. Hell, just about anything is up for grabs with those twins. I used to spend my hard earned dollars to buy the shit I wanted but after hanging with them, I learned a few skills ending up saving a lot of dinero.

After I cleaned up the crib, shit and showered, I got dressed in my BabyPhat jeans and black wraparound shirt. I went to the front door and remote started my Suburban. Those damn things come in handy. When I thought the truck had warmed up enough I locked up the house and was on my way to kick it. I was hoping to see someone interesting instead of the same ol' marks that were in the club every time I went out. It'd be nice to see a new face sprinkled around the crowd.

Heading toward uptown Milwaukee to this club, I was expecting to listen to some good music, see some familiar faces and just hang out and have a good time but I didn't expect to see this dude I always had a crush on from way back in the day named Precious. I called him "P" for short with his fine ass.

This man is six feet tall, caramel complexioned with a beautiful grade of hair on his head. Every time I see him he is always cut up to perfection, sharply dressed and smelling good. But he's always on the move and jittery all the gotdamn time like he's on drugs or something. But I have a natural high so maybe he does too. I hardly ever saw him except for whenever I did decide to step out which is rarely.

For me, going to the club is like packaging myself up to be put on display at a meat market, when my only mission is to go see who I can see and have a good time. I'm like the prime filet choice of meat and the other bitches are just filthy chickens.

Girls are forever wearing skin-tight revealing outfits to get attention from the ballas. And they get that attention too, but I'm not too sure if that attention is really all good. The ballas just wanna hit, quit and forget it. Good thing they know not to step to me like that, that's some shit I don't play. Hmph, now that I think about it that's probably why I'm always alone.

Now as for the ballas, I only have hatred for how they do their business. I hate it when they waste their fast money on frivolous things like car rims, expensive cars, chunky jewelry, gaudy clothes, gold or platinum teeth instead of investing the hard hustled money into something stable and worthwhile like a couple of pieces of real estate or education so they can open up some businesses other than candy stores or pager and cell phone shops. That's what's prevalent here in Milwaukee. On every corner there's a communication shop and candy store. Okay, maybe I'm being a little too hard on them, I suppose they gotta start somewhere because a lot of those shops are owned and operated by foreigners. I know it's hard for brothers to get shit. Banks don't want to lend the money out and so forth. That's what pisses me off about this bullshit ass land. Foreigners get far more play, don't have to pay taxes and for some reason they are only allowed to set up shop in the black communities. I never see them in the white hoods.

Hell, if I hustled the money they did, I'd be straight up unstoppable like a fucking tank. Investments would be on lock and I would have money for play plus money put away for hard times. Now I can't dog all the ballas, just a select few have their heads on straight and doing major thangs while the little hustlers be frontin'. One of my ex- best friends, Shirley met one of the smart ones back in high school and has been with him ever since. His name is Randy and he has a big click of buddies that have their heads on straight. She was down for him since day one and now they are happily married with one child and living it up. Must be nice. Shirley and I aren't friends anymore because she allowed one of her bitch friends to put shit in her head about me wantin' her man. Hell, I wanted a man *like* hers. Never mind the fact that we actually grew up together since grade school. That now dope fiend bitch infiltrated and I will always hate her for it. It hurts that I don't talk to her anymore but life goes on right? Nevertheless, I still miss Shirley.

Another hustler hustled his way from a beeper shop into a franchise sandwich shop. Word is he had to put his businesses in other people's names but nonetheless his shit is legitimate. When money can't be accounted for then a hustla gotta do what they gotta do.

I had exchanged phone numbers with "P" but I was going to see if he was going to actually make the first move and dial my digits but he didn't. After a day or two, I called him and he genuinely sounded surprised to hear from little ol' me. Isn't that special?

We chatted for a short time and he sounds sweet. I can't believe that after all this time, we're actually setting up something to get together tomorrow evening. But with me knowing that he's a major figga nigga we probably won't make it like planned. It always happens like that- make plans and get ready to only get stood up without so much as a courtesy phone call. I hope he don't try to play me like that cuz I may just have to zone out on his fine caramel ass.

I know how I'll play this date thing tomorrow. I'll go on ahead and do what I do but I won't get dressed until I know for sure that we are going to hook up and go out. I'll just lay my clothes to the side and plan to eat something just in case.

I knew he hustled for a living, so that's probably why we didn't get to get together tonight but I would have appreciated a fucking phone call nonetheless. Where do these assholes for men get off thinking that it's cool to not show some kind of responsibility? I got on his ass for that too when I finally did call him and he apologized. Sweet huh? Maybe when we do finally get together we' ll have a good time and kick it. I know his fine ass gotta have at least ten kids, because just looking at him I feel like I'm pregnant.

Back in the day, I remember when I couldn't get *any* play from the fellas. My type wasn't the "in" thing. The "in" thing consisted of being light-skinned with long hair and relatively slim. I am dark complexioned with long hair and my frame was chiseled like Serena Williams, the tennis superstar. I was a black stallion. Additionally, I have full, luscious lips to match. I wasn't the type the guys went for so I was basically alone most of the time.

In time, I blossomed into a chocolate bunny ready to get my hop on. The light skinned fad faded away. The boys would call me a stallion bred from champion lines and that I was, cuz my mother has a body to envy. I was an athlete in high school. I ran track, played basketball, volleyball, and was captain of the cheerleading squad. In shape I was. Then after school my body softened up a bit and I gained a more womanly physique. Though it is kinda hard to find jeans that can encompass my high, round ass to fit properly around my small waist at the same time. Thank goodness for BabyPhat and the FUBU ladies line.

I do know one damn thang, I gotta get "P" in the bed at least once. I always wanted to know what sex would be like with him. I wonder if he's strapped and if he is, does he know what to do with it. It' d be a pity to find out he is and just knows how to fuck like a little young boy. I want a guy who knows how to hit spots from all angles and positions. Work me out, hell. Make me sweat. Make me say your name type shit. Smack me on the ass just right. Shit, make me want to suck your dick after we finished.

So I'll give him a call in a day or two and see if we can hook up and start our affair. We could go out to dinner or something, he seems like the type that likes to eat out a lot. Those pretty ass lips of his are good for more than kissing I just know. Damn my mind is racing. I can imagine him softly kissing me on my lips and commencing me to tongue tusslin'. His hands are soft too, so soft that I can imagine them palming my skin working his hands like a pizza man kneading the dough. I can definitely see myself wrapping my full, soft succulent lips around his erect nipples suckling on each of his breasts like a nursing baby, tenderly sending vibrant nerve sensations coursing down to the tip of his toes. I won't front, I love to suck on a nice size dick too. Deep throatin' is my specialty. I love to suck a dick until I think the skin is about to peel off of it like an overly ripe banana. I've ran into tic tac dicks and couldn't even bring myself to fuck. It can be rough on a single horny sista. Some dicks are like pickles. Those are cool but the ones like big ass cucumbers I can't roll with. I ain't about to allow nan nigga the opportunity tear and rip my insides up. Fuck that. I don't even care for the little ones though but I'll dick the jaw if the nigga's pockets are swoll and he spendin'.

I dream of that perfect fit shit though. Some shit that' ll last for a long while. Trying to play with myself just doesn't cut it. I'm definitely not going to bed just any stud that comes around cuz AIDS is too widespread. I don't even like kissing on different niggas. Ain't no telling where their mouths have been.

I stand firm in my belief that there isn't a sexual person alive in this world male or female that hasn't slipped up and done some unprotected shit especially in the middle of night or during the early morning hard dick phase. I can stand like that because I've allowed it to happen. But I was younger and didn't really think of the dire consequences.

Hell, shit is waay too serious for slip- ups like that to happen to me. I play no games now. Fuck all that.

Hopes Of Tappin'

Dang, what the fuck is taking Jane't so damn long to call me? I just knew she was at least somewhat interested in a playa, balla and part-time hustla like myself. Men do get insecure when a woman doesn't sweat them. But I know she'll call sooner or later.

Finally, like ten years later she decides to call me like I have a lifetime to wait on her, and I don' t. Yes I do. Our conversation was brief but we made plans to hook up tonight to drive over to Chicago to kick it at this place that's like a funhouse for adults. It took damn near two hours to get there and I wanted to swing by my peeps and check them out while in town. I haven't done the family thang in a while.

After visiting my aunt and all, we went to that spot located downtown called Dave & Busters. Milwaukee needs to get something like that downtown somewhere. Jane't and I played video games, basketball, damn near got electrocuted on some game and joked around. I had a lot of pure unadulterated fun.

Sometimes I need to get away from home away from all the hustling.

Hell, don't get me wrong. I love making the money cuz it's quick but sometimes I need time for me. Shit, I wanna go to a spa and get massaged down, a pedicure and maybe even a mud dip, seaweed wrap or something. I'll try that shit out like Blake

Carrington used to do on Dynasty. Real men take care of themselves and their bodies. I ain't ashamed for wanting to do it either.

We walked around downtown Chicago and folks were everywhere. While carousing the streets we noticed some horse drawn carriages so I figure I'd do the playa thang and pay for an excursion on the city streets. Yea, I like this gal. She's pretty cool yet I don't plan on getting attached to her either. I'll kick it with her for a bit and back up off of her cause I'mma always be a playa. The burning question in the back of my head is what if she's the type of woman I've always wanted?

We made it back to Milwaukee not too long afterwards and since I had drove my ride and parked it at her house, I would have to drive home. I was a gentleman and walked her to her door. I told her I would call her once I made it back home. And I did just that. She seems like the type of person I can talk to, only there are things about me that could turn her off but I'll test her on that one day. Until then, I'll just bide my time with her because eventually I will have to move on and that' ll probably hurt her feelings.

Damn, I ain't shit.

As the days progressed we talked and did more things together. This broad was having me do all sort of different types of shit and I'm diggin' it totally. She persuaded me to go this reggae spot down on the eastside. The place was full of college kids and she knew quite a few of them. Now, I'm too cool to be dancing all ova the damn place but I was pulled out onto the dance floor for a hot sec anyway. I knew she had rhythm but damn, she could dance her ass off without even really tryin'. The Rastas were even checkin' her out. I had to sip a couple of beers before I could go out there with her. I'm open to a little bit of change.

Two nights later she met me at one of my favorite restaurants above the Hyatt hotel downtown. We dined on the fine cuisine such as the lamb and she had the duck entrée. Later, we went to a few spots I knew about, played pool and chilled out for a bit. The last spot we were at was my guy' s spot down on east Locust.

My niggas liked her. She knew all the cats there and they all knew her too. One of my guys stepped to me about her. Nothing negative was said. Actually, my guy gave Jane't props. A few more cool points were added to her resume.

While we were there she had kicked my ass in dominoes and played some music on the jukebox. She also told me while we were there that she wanted something of mine like a keepsake or something. Now with me being a man and all I suggested that we go to the hotel and to my surprise she was down with it. I'll give her something of mine all right. I crave to give her my tongue skills and my snake.

I ain't gone lie, I've visualized flicking my tongue softly and methodically over her clitoris while using my fingers to probe her insides hittin' that g-spot. Urban legend has it that we can tell when a woman has some good twat. Looking at Jane't and watching her walk solidified that myth to the hilt. She's thick in the thighs and her ass sits high and round like the character Pam on Martin. Her titties are round and full like grapefruit. Fruit makes me horny. I know suckin' the juice from her pussy will be right. The freak may come out of me and I may even lick her ass. Shit, fuck just knocking the bottom out I wanna paralyze the pussy. She won't be able to piss comfortably when I'm thru with her. I wanna make it so good to her that she won't be able to think straight on the daily basis. My mission is to dick whip her.

I can only imagine how her big lips will feel suckin' on my dick. There's nothing like a woman who gives great brains to set a nigga straight for a couple of days. Size won't be a problem either cuz I'm twerkin' with eight fat inches *and* I know how to work it. I'm not the typical missionary man on top only kind of guy whose only movement is in and out. I put in major work. Figure eight motions are standard for me plus hittin' it from an angle. I'll make sure a woman's shoulders and head are the only thing touching the bed. Elevation is a muthafucka.

Yep, it's going to go down for real. I get a kick outta makin' a woman climb the walls in the pursuit of safety from this anaconda. Good dick keeps a woman on line and in line. A lot of women will let a man trample all over them but if the Johnson is good, everything is gravy.

I can only imagine lapping at that pussy like a kitten thirsty for some milk. I'm extremely skilled at feather flicking.

New cell numbers are a staple in my life. A playa used to get hounded too much. Women can appreciate the kind of man that doesn't handle the clit too rough. What most men need to learn is that just sticking the tongue in and out the pussy isn't enough.

It's an art to eating pussy not just the prelude to tappin' that ass. I should teach sex education somewhere in someone's basement.

Horny Ain't The Word

Wow, Precious and me have been kickin' it and I'm having a blast too. I'll show him off on any given day, any given time, and any given place cuz he is just that damn fine. I told him earlier tonight that I wanted something of his to have and he suggested we go to a hotel. OK.

I bet he was a little taken aback that I knew his balla buddies and they all were cool with me. I know a lot of people in this city and they know me. I'm glad I have a cool ass reputation, never a chickenhead. That's definitely something to be proud of too.

We went to the Hyatt located downtown. In the room, we watched some tv, then we both took showers and chilled out on the bed but I wanted to kiss the shit outta him. I hate it when men front like they all cool and laidback knowing damn well they want to get at me in every way possible. I'm a vixen.

After a while finally, his lips found their way to mine and in a long passionate soft kiss I really could tell how badly he wanted me. When my lips parted a jolt of pleasure rippled through my body as his tongue searched for mine. I couldn't help but to wrap my arms around his neck and caress his head with my fingers. While running my hands along his body I could feel his muscles tense and twitch and the scars from his being shot back in the day. Thing is, I wanted him for more than just one measly night; I wanted him for many nights. Deep down somehow I knew that wouldn't be possible, so I made the resolve to take what I could get while it lasted.

As we shared more hot tongue-twisting kisses, he pulled away to remove his towel. He continued to kiss me, driving me crazy as his head casually dipped south to my ample breasts and nipples. Precious suckled each tittie with mad skills making my back arch. On his continued journey south, I experienced his tongue twirling around my navel. Damn, if only you could know the feelings I was feeling about this bad boy. His pretty lips found their way to my wet, juicy twat and I was hoping he knew what to do cuz a sista has had her share of bad dining before.

I helped the bruh out by spreading my brown sugar walls for him to have full access to my womanhood. He lapped and suckled like a hungry tiger eating its fallen prey. He was searching hard for the pink pearl of my oyster. But when he did find it, the pink pearl was manipulated so lightly that I had thoughts of returning the favor. Yea, I wanted to wrap my big lips around the head of his dick and take him all in my mouth with one slowly controlled movement. Shiid, I wanted to suck the skin off his dick but he wouldn't allow it. At least on this particular evening he wouldn' t. Oh well, I'll get at him another time and when I do, his toes will curl toward his knees cuz a bitch is bad when it comes to dickin' the jaws. If he keeps dining out on me the way he is I'm going to have to take control and go for what I know.

I ain't no punk in the bed either. Hell, when I get to gyratin' on a dick with my figure eight motions and squeezing my Kegel muscles men's faces get to contorting. Doing the hoola-hoop moves that that comedian Sommore talks about on the Queens of Comedy have the toes bent up too. Swoosh-a-swoosh, swoosh-a- swoosh. I know my snatch was tight and wet, hell I haven't fucked anyone in months and it was due time, especially with this fine specimen. Ok, I haven't had sex with a man in some months that is. I'll get back to that later.

From the looks of it, he appears to be an eight incher and only my higher power knows that I hope he knows what to do with it. Hell, I haven't fucked in months. Puleeze, grant me the blessing that he knows what to do with it.

When he finally positioned himself to enter me he did so slowly and methodically. With every thrust he made I squeezed my pussy muscles and bore down into the bed. Through gasps of air, Precious huskily whispered in my ear how good, tight and wet I felt to him. I let him know that it was time to switch to my favorite position, doggy style. He took his time stroking me from the back not wanting to nut too quickly I gather. That was a good thing too because I wanted to ride his dick like I was a professional jockey. As I mounted my stallion I took notice of the fuck faces he was making. Damn, he looks good. As I contracted my muscles giving him my all I knew he was digging my skills too. Shit, after ten minutes of that my legs were getting tired as hell (mental note: do more squats). The intensity of our bodies grinding together rocketed him to an overpowering sensation and with one final thrust he nutted in me. Well, actually in the condom.

I don't climax, never have but I do feel very sorry for the poor lad that does have the ability to lay it down on me. I may turn into psycho woman. Stalker. Headhunter. Whatever you want to call it. All I know is that it'll be crucial if the poor guy tried to leave a sista. I can see the headlines now: Sex really can kill.

Later into that night, we chitchatted about our lives and doze off to sleep. As I was drifting off, I came to the realization that trying to be in Precious' s life extensively could be the death of me. Emotionally. I've been on enough roller coasters to know I don't care to be on a new one. He's in the game a bit too much it seems.

The following morning I dropped him off at home on 26th street and he sent me off with a kiss. I hope we can continue to get together and kick it like we've been doing. Hell, I need a little excitement in my life for a change. One thing is for sure, sex changes everything in any relationship for the good or the bad.

I've met millionaire ballas who like to think that just because they have a reputation for having money that my legs would spread easily for them. First of all, I don't give up the pussy for nuthin' unless I want to. Second of all, a nigga's bank doesn't mean that he' ll hand me some of it.

In fact, a multi-million dollar balla had the nerve to just come out and tell me that he needed me for some pussy. Hell, I told him that I needed a four family apartment building in my name.

Don't think that fool didn't shut the fuck up. Asking me for pussy is like taking out a contract with me. I play no games, it ain't no open season between these legs. No one is just going to be layin' up in this ass for nuthin'.

Grown Realizations

Recalling childhood, I can remember when I had a crush on someone and butterflies would roam around in my gut and that is happening now when I think of Precious. But I must remember that fucking with a man in his position won't care to be with a woman on her terms especially when that man can have new pussy on the daily.

Oh geez, I think I'm already in love with him and it ain't because of the good fuckin' either. I always liked him ever since I first saw him way back in the day. Am I wrong for that? Maybe I shouldn't have given him the ass so soon, but damn, I know what I wanted.

I don't consider myself to be a hoe or a loose woman but I have needs too. I get damn tired of fantasizing about the perfect lover. I hate it when society puts the stigma on women to be virtuous while the men can act out like loose cannons fuckin' everything in sight, slangin' dick with the community.

I've had to come to the conclusion that yes, I am a grown ass woman. Yes, I do get horny as hell. Yes, I only have one life to live and I need to live it. Yes, I don't have to answer to anyone other than myself. Yes, I can fuck anyone regardless of gender I damn well please. Yes, I got it like that.

Yep.

I came to all of those conclusions and am learning to stand by them. If men can have their fun, well gotdammit I can too! But it'll cost most of time.

Bitch Apprehension

My night with Jane't was nice from beginning to the end. Since she told me she's never had an orgasm I was hoping to accomplish that mission when we finally had sex. She had also forewarned me that whoever the lucky guy was who did manage to help her cum would have a hard time getting rid of her. But for some reason or another, I wanted her hooked to me anyway. I may be playing a dangerous game with her. I already know she's the violent type. I did my homework.

The violent types of females are the ones who are super cool and calm yet they have a short fuse for a temper. She looks like the type that will fuck a nigga up royally for playing with her feelings. Her eyes are so damn big and sexy that when she looks at me it feels as if she's burning a hole through me. A bruh gotta be leery of those kinds of eyes.

Well, I have some business I need to tend to today. I avoided all my phone calls yesterday and I know Kelly was one of those calls. I'll just tell her I didn't have any juice on my celly. I'll set up something with her for later on today or tomorrow.

Being a playa is hard. You always have to juggle around the women you mess with, and while your at it, making a conscientious effort to not get caught up or call any of them the wrong name. I did that one time talking over the telephone and boy oh boy, if that girl was in the same room with me, I doubt it that I would still have my front teeth or one of my natural eyeballs.

Some broads don't know how to act and lose focus on containing themselves. Composure can be lost in a matter of seconds when feelings are involved so I try to tread lightly.

I kinda like being a free Willy mutha. I can get with whomever I feel like, whenever. No strings attached.

Hell, I've been fortunate enough to meet a coupla true playerettes. I'll be with a shorty and get a phone call or two from some others and the playerette won't say a word. Then when I hang up she won't even mention it or act funny. I like that in a broad. That just lets me know that I can kick it however with her and she'll play her part like she's going for an Emmy.

I know I may have hurt some women with that plus I truly believe I got drama to pay for one day when *that* one woman comes along.

Karma is janky like that. The infamous boomerang effect could have a muthafucka running around in circles.

Hookin' It Up

Back at the ranch, Phyllis was doing much better and enjoying her newly remodeled home. Now it was time to remodel the lower level. The house was somewhat similar in the total design but instead of pale yellow marble in the kitchen I had a peach color installed and plain white appliances to add some serenity to the kitchen. I bought a marble topped island to match the marble topped counters to sit in the center of the kitchen floor. My bathroom was also enlarged and a custom black sink, tub and toilet were installed. I had the floor decorated with an all black ceramic marble tile.

Being that I'm a man, instead of having a chaise lounge in my bathroom I decided to put a 32" flatscreen tv in the wall. My tub faced the television so I wouldn't have to worry about catching whiplash. I shall be king of my castle. Hell, I gotta have a comfortable place to shit.

Kelly went shopping for some Italian leather furniture for the living room and we both picked out a four-poster king-size bed set from Eddie Bauer. I don't require too much because it's just me, yet and still a nigga gone be comfortable. She wanted to go and cop me some pieces from Ethan Allen furniture to go with the bedset. The dining room can remain empty for now but I'm still gonna have a grand chandelier put up. I might just need to put a baby grand piano in the dining room. I don't know how to play a lick on the damn thing but its cool to have it just for status. Then again I may just may take up some lessons and do a Brian McKnight on someone. Who says people in the hood can't live the lifestyles of the rich and fucking filthy famous?

The last step in morphing the house into a castle is to put new siding on the house. Mom and I need to make a journey to Sears to pick two colors out or have a representative come out and show us some material. Once that's completed, I can sit my ass down, design an outlay and ponder on how I'm going to hook up the basement. I do know for a fact that I want a pimpish ass pool table and three large fish tanks. One tank will house a shark, another some piranha and the third will be full of exotic strange looking fish. One of the tanks will be put in the bottom middle of the bar I plan on having installed.

I need to have secret compartments down there in the basement to stash my grip and other important private shit. So far everything' s going smoothly but that's no cause for me to slack off. Gotta do this shit while I'm able to while maintaining my square.

Later on, I suppose I can go pay a visit to El better known in the streets as Onyx and his mom today, I haven't seen them in over a week being so busy with these women and the house. Blue will be proud of my accomplishments on the house. I just may have to have a housewarming party with a few invited close guests. It's never a wise idea to let too many folks see how you're living and where you lay your head. It's crazy trying to learn how to trust people nowadays. I'd hate to get burnt again.

I know a fool that was stupid enough to let everybody and they momma come to his flat to only get burglarized that next week. He didn't have a clue as to where to start looking for the perpetrators because there' d been so many damn people at his spot. He had alarms on everything but if it's any one group of people that *know* how to get around security shit, its niggas. I wouldn't be surprised if the jackals who did it had sat to ate with the man at his table or even used his toilet.

Hoe Killing

Over the past couple of weeks, Jack had been satisfying his sick pleasures in the comfort of his motel room. From reading an adult entertainment newspaper that came out every two weeks, he was able to summon the services of various call girls for his bizarre carnal desires. Upon contacting a particularly attractive white female that went by the name of Sugar, he was able to set up an appointment with the contracted whore.

Her advertisement had her actual picture in it. Sugar stood to be about five seven, weighing one hundred and forty pounds with brown shoulder length hair and hazel eyes. The bitch wore a size forty DD bra thanks to her five thousand dollar tit job. She worked at the local strip joints in the city but also moonlighted on the side with her escort gigs for even more money. She was definitely ' bout gettin' bread.

Jack had made the stipulation that she would have to don a mask depicting the likeness of a black woman during their session and he would gladly pay her a fee of three hundred dollars for a half-hour of time.

At first she was taken aback by his request because even though she had performed requests of pissing and shittin' on johns, fucking them in the asses, beatin' the shit outta them and other thangs of that nature, never before had she been asked to wear a mask. But to be asked to wear a mask of a black woman was even stranger yet for a quick three hundred dollars she'll wear that muthafucka all day as long as he paid for it by the half hour.

Jack couldn't get a hard-on like any normally functioning fucking male. He only got on rock when he fantasized or was about to actually fuck a black girl. He had to use his imagination for shit like that or else it just wouldn't work. Therefore, for Sugar to wear a mask with the depiction of a black woman was absolutely essential. No worry about the rest of her body being exposed without having color while in the act of copulating because they would be underneath the sheets in the dim hotel light. Out of sight out of mind.

Sugar would see Jack on a weekly basis, sometimes up to three times per week. In the third week, the calculating mentally ill muthafucka juked out.

During the sodomistic attack, Jack blacked out and really believed he was with a black whore. He rammed his dick inside the walls of Sugar' s anus causing skin tissue to rip and blood to seep out her asshole. If she were awake the pain would have been intolerable. It's not like Sugar could scream out for help. She had drank a special concoction Jack had made for her that included the date rape drug. Jack went so far as to painting the girl with brown latex paint before he began his sadistic rite.

He had been laying low in Milwaukee since killing Passionfruit and instead of roaming the streets of Milwaukee he traveled to other clubs up north in the state to see who was working where.

It's not like he couldn't mingle wherever he went. He was able to fit in anywhere he went. How many people are really going to eyeball an average looking and acting white man?

Before he left the motel room he was residing at, he made sure to clear the place of any of his fingerprints and any other crucial evidence that could link him to the rental of that room. Jack has been in this game for a while and knew not to ever rent a room in his true identity. He also knew to bring strong industrial cleaning supplies to wipe down the fixtures. As for as deoxyribonucleic acid was concerned being on the sheets, he took extra precaution by laying thick plastic over the entire bed and sleeping on a his own mattress cover. Hotel rooms are incredibly nasty anyhow but he cared to not leave any residue of any kind behind.

When Sugar finally came to, she felt something was terribly wrong with her; excruciating pain enveloped her entire body as the effects of the drug slowly wore off. Upon opening her eyes, her vision was blurred and she had a horrible headache. Every time she tried to move a part of her body it felt as if whatever muscle she attempted to use was weighed down by a twenty pound weight. Thirty minutes later, she was able to muster up enough strength to get by telephone. Sad thing is, she couldn't use the motel phone to dial out 911 cause the jack had been removed from the security of the wall plus the cord was severed in half. Mustering all the strength she had left in her weary body she crawled out of the room onto the walkway of the motel and moaned for help. Luckily, a motel employee was conducting a last round of duties before taking off for home and spotted the poor chile laying in the fetal position. The fire department and police were called immediately. Sugar was lightly examined on the scene and later after some brief questioning taken to the hospital for further observation and treatment. Tests were performed and DNA was sampled and collected. Apparently Jack didn't have the smarts to use a condom while sodomizing her. When she had the strength and the antidote to the drugs she was given had balanced out, she was able to give a description of her attacker and the details of their meeting.

Normally cops don't give a damn about working girls or their plights of safety but being that she was a white woman they gave her case extra *special* attention. A profile sketch artist came to the hospital and a drawing was made of the suspect. All the news stations covered this story and displayed the sketch drawing of the suspect on television.

Meanwhile, Jack was on his way up north to one of the strip clubs he paid a visit to a few days prior where he saw two very cute black girls working at. He had followed the girls to the motel they were staying at and took notice of how they handled their business during the days and their action at night. He was almost able to get one of the girls to come to his car one evening but she wouldn't walk over to where he was parked. The young black girl wanted him to come to her instead. Perhaps another time that'll happen he reasoned.

So in the meantime, he decided to call an escort service requesting a dominatrix. When the girl arrived, he played the role of a submissive male for a while before he viciously attacked her. Beating her senseless as if she were a man he ultimately knocked her unconscious. Jack shot some drugs up in her system and dismembered parts of her body.

The first body parts he chopped off her body were her hands. Placing the amputated hands atop the back of the toilet, it appeared that the hands were similar to being towel holders. He then chopped off one of her feet with the wooden axe.

His sickening brutality continued well off into the late evening. Methodically slicing the toes from the other foot he casually tossed the five extensions about the room, placing the remainder of the foot in between the victims ass cheeks.

That saying "I'll break my foot off up in your ass" is truly a muthafucka.

Jack' s ways were becoming more profound and sickly as the days went by.

Pimp Beginnings

Word on the street was that Loc was going to be indicted on federal drug charges. Hell, charges like that carries damn near a life sentence. If that happens, he' ll no definitely have to do his time in another state facility out of state.

Damn, that also means that I could be implicated in the sting and that's some shit I definitely don't need. Muthafuckas stay gettin' caught up on conspiracy charges. It's bad enough niggas out here blabbin' and flappin' off at the mouth about the game. Every other day some bitch ass nigga is snitchin' to stay out here in the streets. I already know someone is bound to blab to the peoples about Loc and all of us who deal with him.

Now I have to figure out away to wean myself from him, figure out a way I can keep my money steadily flowin', while maintaining my living status. There' s nothing worse than going from having money to not having it at all. That's like rollin' a Benzo one day to getting knocked down to a Pacer the following week. I've seen one too many cats doin' their thang having their way to getting locked up and losing everything they hustled for and then some. Or when worse come to worse, some of the same money having ballas ended up using their own product and fallin' off.

Ahhh! I suppose I could take El up on his offer to start me off with a few girls, what could it hurt. I could use the easy money. Let's see, if I can get two or three good looking girls on my team I could easily pull in more than ten thousand a month. I'll just have to always keep one in the brothels in Nevada, one in the houses here, and the other one in the strip clubs out of town. Most girls that want to hoe only want to keep their hair and nails done plus dress fly every day. Straightup chickenheads. Then there are the jumpdowns that'll get down to make they nigga look fly. Those are the types that have no focus at all. They walk around looking dizzy all the damn time. I have to wonder though do they *ever* sit back and think about all the money they copped and what possibly could've been done with it all?

I'll even get each of them a two-way pager so we all can keep in touch with each other the high-tech way. I can see myself being the type to spoil my harem. El could probably fix me up with one or two tonight. I'd rather have happy hookers on my team than disgruntled ones.

Driving along, the usual was going on down on Wisconsin avenue and I could see a few of El's girls on the hoe stroll. I walked into his spot and commenced to jackin' with him. I told him of my future plans to get inducted into the pimp game and he was diggin' it. We had set an appointment for later that evening around ten o'clock. He already had a girl in mind for me. I hope she's cute enough to pull in some real bread for a playa. If she's good and doesn't have a stable place to live, I may have to let her stay with me for a while until I find a few more hotties and can cop them a pad to lay their heads and rest their weary feet. Whoever pulls in the most bank and can show me the most utmost loyalty will be my bottom hoe.

A bottom hoe is the bitch that keeps her ears, eyes, and brain closed while popping that pussy the best. When a hoe tries to get out of line or clip some bread away for a personal stash the bottom will handle that and let the pimp know the real. In situations like that, one of two thangs can happen the most popular one of all is the beatdown.

One pimp in the Mil, D-Bone, was known for beating the dog shit outta one of his bitches with a bat and phone book to only then make the poor gal sit in a tub full of ice cubed water. The girl had to sit in that tub until a cigarette burned itself out on a toilet top. If she moved to try to get the tub, she opened herself up to get beat some more.

This same pimp would fuck any of his girls in the ass as punishment for gettin' out of line.

I heard from a trusty source that the girl had black and purple bruises all over her body. Apparently, she was too afraid to leave the brutal guy.

This gorilla was well known for huntin' and chasin' down his hoes whenever they tried to leave him even for another pimp. Where dude messed up at though, he was trying to sell dope and pimp at the same time. From what I heard, pimping is a full time job that requires constant guidance and trap checking.

This new gig will keep me floatin' for a while and if it's all to the good I won't have to touch dope ever again. Besides, I'm not attempting to send myself nor allow anyone else to send me to prison.

From the looks of El and Blue, pimpin' is a sure thing. Drug cases carry automatic ten-year sentences nowadays and I'm not trying to sit in anyone's jail day after day thinking of ways I could have done shit differently. No way, no how.

Since I have a couple of hours on my hand until the meeting with El, I can call up Kelly to get in her business for a little while.

Luckily, she was preparing a small dinner of scalloped cheese potatoes, oven barbecued chicken, Caesar salad and hard rolls. I haven't eaten too much of anything all day anyhow so I will be going to get my grub on. A bruh needs to eat too yanno.

Kelly is a sweetheart and I wonder if there' s an underlying reason for it. As loaded as she is, I still don't understand why she feels the continuous need to hustle like she does.

Looking at her, she would make a lot of money in the prostitution circle. I can see her working for a high-class escort service getting paid by affluent rich white men. The broads that do make close to $4000 a week if not more and sex isn't even part of the plan most of the times. I know she digs me, so maybe I can try to sneak the subject in on her in conversation tonight at dinner.

I arrived at Kelly' s house at about a quarter to nine. Just walking in her house made me feel like I was at a botanical garden. Fresh flowers were everywhere. I wonder are her flowers delivered every other day or was this just for show.

The dinner was cool, it certainly didn't taste like a black woman cooked it. She was dressed in pink silk loungewear and through the fabric I could see her body' s curves. A very shapely woman she is I thought.

Now my timing for the important conversation must be exact in its calculation. I know if I brought it up at the wrong time things would be jeopardized for the worst. People always say timing is important in certain predicaments.

After dinner, we sat on her floor cushioned by large Indonesian pillows and rugs. The music of Luther was playing nearby in the background. I had asked Kelly what were some things she definitely wouldn't do for money.

Surprisingly enough, paid sex wasn't one of them to my delight. So I knew then that it would be cool to bring it up now at this point. I let her know that a lot of good money could be made escorting and she wouldn't have to forge checks and credit cards anymore for fun. I also mentioned to her that if she would be interested in that type of employment we could have that info faxed to us. Agencies are good for getting the clientele up and going.

After dealing with a trick, the middleman could be cut out and that would mean more profit for the girl. Some tricks want to marry the whore they like and take complete care of them. One thing is for certain, there are no surprises on whether or not a woman wants love or money. So we trekked through cyberspace and looked up a gazillon agencies and requested that they send us some info. We got information from at least 12 good agencies throughout the states and even from a few out of the country.

We also received some information from a few escort agencies in town; some based out of Hollywood and Florida that would have her work here in the Midwest. One agency was Babydolls out of Hollywood. That agency catered mainly to the stars and a beautiful girl like Kelly could easily make ten grand a week. I knew this already because I had sent a couple of her pictures in for them to evaluate when I first met her. One snapshot was of her in a bikini when we were at the Hyatt downtown in the jacuzzi room and the other snapshot was of her dressed in a pinstripe short skirt suit. It's always good to have a broad that can go from corporate classy to slutty trashy just like Superman changed to Clark Kent in a matter of seconds.

Kelly resembles Charlie the actress to a tee. Height, weight, eyes, hair, everything is practically exact. Well ...her ass is slightly larger. Babydolls fee for sending each girl out is one-third of what's charged per outing. The least a john can spend with one of their babes is fifteen hundred dollars. During the Grammys and Oscars is when they are at their busiest. Most girls get tipped an extra few thousand dollars. Tricks come straight out the pocket or off the credit card during major events like those.

The agency based out of Florida, Executive Escorts, cater to the CEO businessmen, doctors, attorneys, engineers and music execs. To meet with clients, they' ll fly their girls anywhere within the country to handle business, whatever it was. Flying expenses, hotel, meals and transportation fees aren't all-inclusive and must be taken care of by the john. Depending on the location, those fees could range from five hundred to a thousand dollars alone. The men don't mind paying for those fees either. They make so much damn money the fees aren't an issue for them. Some girls spend a weekend with the tricks or just one day. The least money some of their girls make a week is five thousand dollars.

Sometimes I wish I were a woman. I'd be one rich bitch, calling shots and runnin' thangs. Pussy controls. Pussy is power. It doesn't take a rocket scientist to figure it out.

If I can convince Kelly to be down with me, I would have to make her my bottom. Not because of love but because of the fact that once she's making that type of money, I wouldn't want her to run off and leave my black ass for any of those johns. Who knows? I would probably make her have my baby too. Women are dedicated to their children if they have some class and respect for themselves. I believe she's that type. After our talk I told her to think about it overnight and I would call her tomorrow for her answer and she could get started next week.

Now it was ten o' clock and I needed to make my way over El's house to see the girl he was going to sic on me. When I arrived I couldn't help but to see Blue' s car parked down the street. She must be visiting, that's good for me too because I can now ask her to keep her eye out for another government house I could rehab. This next house I plan to get will either get resold or rented to someone on government assistance. Folks on assistance guarantees my rent being paid for up to a year without delay. Sure, they may fuck up the place here and there but I'd rather take my chances on some for sure money than up in the air or sometimes late money. I may be lucky enough to rent out to a decent young woman that possesses class and integrity. Maybe someone I could fuck.

Music was blaring from El's crib and the lights were on everywhere. I wondered who was inside. When I finally walked in I saw a small gathering of what looked like family members. They keep in touch through various means.

El beckoned for me to follow him to another spot in the house. We went down in the basement where a few of his employees were. He led me to the table and asked for a girl named Ivory and a girl named Cashmere to come out the back room. Ivory was a pretty young girl, mixed with both Indian and white, she had long dark hair and high cheekbones. She didn't have an ass at all and her breasts were on the smaller side.

Older men like young girls like that. The tricks like to think they're messing with fresh meat instead of experienced whores. El copped her carrying a backpack and looking lost and lonely downtown at the Greyhound bus station. She has no family here that she's aware of. She ran away from home because of the sexual abuse she suffered at the hands of her father' s girlfriend.

The story with that is, whenever her father left the house the girlfriend would incite small talk and become very touchy feely. The shit hit the fan one day when the girlfriend forced the girl's legs open after she was coming out the shower and went down on her right on the hallway floor.

More incidents similar to that took place even to the point of the girlfriend donning a strap on and penetrating the girl while she was asleep one early morning. Ivory couldn't take the abuse anymore after that so she made preparations to runaway that same week.

Not knowing where she was going, she just used her savings, hopped on the Greyhound and got off wherever her ticket took her, which ended up being Milwaukee. Not knowing whether or not she had any family here, she was broke, homeless, and hungry.

She was just cool with not being at home with all the bullshit. Cashmere was a chocolate delight. She's tall, slim, and scarless with big doe eyes and medium length hair. She's model material and nineteen with dimples. Her body was built like Halle Berry' s and she walks with a graceful air about herself.

El copped her at a strip club near Villard Avenue. I swear that strip club is the worst but it employs some decent looking girls from time to time.

I can tell she's a quiet girl, I wonder what made her want to dance instead of trying to get with the Ebony Fashion Fair modeling circuit. The girl has got to be about five eleven without heels. Perhaps this is just a stepping-stone for her.

The word on Cash is that she was fresh out of high school and on her way to college when a family crisis put her in the position of having to come up with some quick bread. Working a job paying five dollars an hour didn't appeal too much to her so she summoned up the courage to get a pair of heels and a bathing suit. Not wanting to go out of town just yet, she went and applied to work at the club and was hired immediately. Faced with receiving a minimum wage check and tips she was able to pull about five hundred a week. Good money for a nineteen year old to pull.

After seeing to it that her family was back on the right track she opened a savings account and accumulated a net worth of about five thousand dollars. I see potential in this child. If all goes well with Kelly and Ivory, I'll be a good guy and see what I can do to help her break into that business of modeling. I may just have to become her personal manager.

The girls were eager to begin work, so I got on the horn and made two bookings up in Black River Falls. The club I'm sending them to pays $350 a week and they have to sell drinks. The money is good up there so I know they should be able to pull about $2000 from there. They both can work up there for the next two weeks and they have to leave Sunday on the bus to get there in time Monday. Since today is Friday, I have time to get their hair done, pedicures and manicures.

For the beginning of their employment with me, I'll buy them both ten new complete outfits to dance in with two pair of shoes. Blue gets dance outfits at wholesale and I would only have to spend three hundred. An outfit that would cost a hundred dollars at the dance store would only run me half of that, and the shoes that would cost one hundred would really only run about forty bucks so I can get a lot for three hundred dollars. The girls already had a few outfits decent enough to work in.

I need to go downtown and cop a business name so I can buy that shit for a little bit of nothing on my own. She always helps me when I ask her to. I'll get that change back when the girls come from their working vacation. If they come correct, I'll treat them both to a nice dinner at the steakhouse, movie and a night of clubbing at the hotspot.

Most pimps I know only like for their girls to work, work, and work. Those hoes appearances take a serious beating for not getting adequate rest. The concept of getting' that money up ain't too bad, however, I believe the girls should get a break and be able to enjoy themselves every once in a while to keep them happy and more willing to work.

I told Ivory and Cashmere I would be there to pick them up early tomorrow so it's for them to get some rest tonight and be ready to roll out.

Secret Yearnings

My demons get at me from time to time and controlling them can be quite the chore. You can call it what you want or even describe it as you wish but lemme get one thang straight …I AM NOT HOMOSEXUAL!

When I was much younger I had had a few experiences here and there with my mother' s boyfriend, involuntarily mind you. And from those experiences I have developed a craving for getting my dick sucked by men. I ain't gone lie, I fucked a hole or a few and the feeling was great.

Being a respected drug pusher and feared leader of the streets it's not too cool to be known for having fetishes like mine.

Everything I do that pertains to the other side has to be done on the low down or all sorts of bullshit could blow up in my face. My niggas wouldn't want to fuck with me if they knew.

In the past few years, I have only been dealing with one man who I refer to as "Sweets". I can't even begin to front on him the man is fine. He's a tall drink of chocolate milk towering at six four with a nice grade of naturally curly hair. His eyes are light brown and he has deep dimples in his cheeks. My downlow squeeze keeps his hair cut in 360 waves and he always keeps his appearance up to par. The cologne he wears is the fragrance I bought for him to spritz his body with. Built like a linebacker he can fill an expensive suit out GQ style not missing a beat.

I met him in Chicago at one of the windy city's hotspots for those in the life. I travel up there now and then to get away from all the bullshit I encounter back here at home- the hoes, the illegitimate job of being a pharmacist, my girl, the snitches the whole nine. I just gotta get away sometimes.

Now don't get me wrong, I'm not homosexual, but I am only am attracted to the kind of men that look good and are masculine. I don't care for the sissy muthafuckas a' ight? My nigga Sweets lives a double life just like I do. He has a woman at home that he's been with for over three years. But like him, I have my secret desires that gotta be fulfilled.

Women always complain about having issues with men on the downlow for good reason. I say that because many of us *are* on the downlow and the unsuspecting women in our lives have no fucking clue that when they kiss us, they also kiss our lovers. When they slurp and slobber on our dicks, they don't know that our dicks have been in another man's mouth and/or ass. Crude? Yea, it is. Yet, what can be done about it? I've tried to fight my emotions about this shit but it doesn't help any. Society got me all fucked up in the head and I can't help but to keep a migraine. True to life, my girl would be totally wrecked if she ever found out about my secret bidness and she doesn't deserve that kind of pain. Keeping the business under wraps is crucial to my well being because if word ever leaked out about me, I could possibly find myself cut the hell up into slivers of skin. It is becoming a chore handling two relationships on two different levels because most of the time, I just don't want to be around my bitch. I can't truly pinpoint how or why, but sometimes I just feel closer to Sweets than to my future child's mother who I've been with the past half a decade. Just like women have their special bonds with each other, we men have our manly bonds with one another. Some bonds a lil' more personal than normal. Like women we talk about the latest gossip too. We gripe to each other about our home situations.

Sometimes we speak on our money matters. We definitely speak on our bitch issues.

Please don't get me wrong I love my wifey. She's been down with me for the longest and never has she tried to play me. She's been down with me since day one. I can remember when I didn't have shit compared to what I have now. Ain't shit really changed in the hood but my bankrolls. I got no choice but to hold my cabbage together with rubberbands. Pussy ain't eva been a problem for me cuz as long as I got my rep and the greens to back it up, stank hoes come a nickel a dozen. I've more than my share of pussy, some good some bad. That shit gets played. Quick.

I know plenty of niggas who dealt with broads that were perpetrating frauds. They would cheat on them, steal from the stash and even go so far as to set them up for the ultimate street hustlers treason: the in house robbery. My girl has always been true to life so there' s not too much I wouldn't do for her. She deserves the best that life has to offer and for as long as I've been hustling she's enjoyed the fruits of my labors. I know that she would be extremely devastated if she found out about my secret life. Do I love her? Yes. Would I kill for her? Yes. Would I marry her? Yes. Would I lie to her? Yes. A truth like that could make her go overboard. She could go crazy, lose her mind, shoot her marbles or just damn straight take me out of my living misery.

One thing always shown to me in my family is that a woman can be seriously dangerous especially once she's scorned. They say hell hath no fury. I've witnessed my sisters do some twisted off the wall type of shit to some of the men in their lives.

On the flip side, I know I could never have a fully blown relationship with Sweets. If word got out about his other life, the news could scar his career. The nigga is a pro-basketball player with a more promising chance of upping his stakes in the game. He's in negotiations about improving his contract with the team. Don't get it confused, he's definitely not the only bisexual in the league but that's another story.

Facing this case against me, I may end up doing some major time. I'm happy to know that due to my common sense I invested a substantial amount of money into businesses that are fail proof. My newborn baby won't ever have to do without. Now even though I love my baby' s momma, my own moms advised me to take out a life insurance policy on myself for my child in the event something foul happened to me. I could make it to that when my baby turns eighteen, only my child can touch the money from the policy.

Yall know just like I do that when a woman has money at her disposal, she'll clown and floss while the child has to do with far too little than allowable. I know girls that get money from my guys and turn around and cop new cars, clothes and jewelry instead of taking care of business. I don't honestly believe that my girl is a rat like that but hey you can be with a person for fifty years and not really know them. She *is* a project hoe.

Well, I suppose I'll give Sweets a call, I wouldn't mind being in his company for a few hours. I need some attention from him. Shit, driving nearly two hours just to see him would give me some peaceful quiet time to myself to sort out some thoughts about this game called life.

Imaginin' him bear hugging me smellin' all good and shit gets my dick jittery. I can't wait for him to fondle me in all the places that turn me on. For some reason, I want to suck his dick dry of any fluids running along inside of it. I need to hear him moan. I need for him to hear me moan when he engulfs my piece with his wet mouth. His suction skills are off the chain.

In fact, I wanna go the whole nine yards with him. Why all of a sudden I'm developing these yearnings beats the shit outta me but I just know that I have to have him totally, in my mouth, in my arms, in my ass.

Don't act like this shit doesn't happen cause it truly does on the daily in every city, suburb, hotel, school and wherever else.

Hmph, someone you know even gets down with the get down. Virtual reality. I'm tired of being sick and tired.

I'll have come up with the excuse to my girl that I have business to take care in the Windy city. She never questions me when it comes to business as long as she's taken care of and doesn't want for anything everything is cool as ice. I dialed his cell phone.

"Say Sweets it's me, what's up?"

"Hey man all is good with me, what's up, do you wanna come down here?"

"Yea, I could really go for spending some quality time with you for a few hours you game?"

"Sure my man. I need to have some time with you too. I have some frustrations that I think you could help me unleash. I'll get a room for us downtown at the InterContinental, how soon will you get here?"

"I'm on my way in about half an hour."

"Word, I'll holla atcha when you touch down."

As Loc prepared to take his journey to his secret lover, he had to think of yet another crafty excuse to tell his woman about why he couldn't be back home for dinner.

Congrats

Driving home, I stopped off at Rob's Lounge on Lisbon to have a drink. A few of the hood gangbangers were in attendance so I hung out with them jackballin' and playing pool.

Loc stepped up in the place not to long after I did and he just didn't look quite right. He had lost some weight and looked worried about something. Either that, or he was snorting his work on the side.

A lot of dealers always ended up on their own product after serving a while in the game. Ballers ended up snortin' so much shit that all the lining in their noses deteriorated causing unexpected nosebleeds. Niggas be mentally disturbed. Loc was properly greeted and hung with all of us for a while before the bar closed.

I bounced and was on my way to the flat when an old girl of mine, LaQuanda called my cell phone. We haven't spoken to each other in over six weeks, and I can't really recall how we lost touch but we did. She just called to say hi and to invite me to her birthday bash at a spot on Atkinson Street Saturday night. She'll be twenty-three and this will also be her going away to college party. She was accepted into a historically black college in Atlanta and she was moving there permanently.

A real man should always be proud of a woman when she's out to better herself whether she's doing it the slow way or the fast way. Moving out of Milwaukee may be a good deal for her, nothing too much happens up here anyway. I guess I'll stop in and show my face and give my congrats for about an hour or so tomorrow night. The party starts at nine o' clock. To show my respect for her and her family I'll be donning a suit.

Sometimes I think I need to further my education myself. Phyllis would be proud of me if I did that instead of running the streets everyday hustling to make a dolla outta a dime and nickel. I'll take up some real estate classes and become a broker, that should only take about three months to complete, and I know I can do that and still handle my biz with the girls. The more productive

I can be will only net benefits in the long run.

Damn, I forgot Loc needed to holla at me about something. I better call him before the night is over. I also get to find out Kelly' s answer tomorrow about the escort agencies. I haven't thought about Jane't all day too busy running around and she hasn't called me either. Oh well, I'll get around to her.

Waking up to the smells of bacon, onion cheese eggs, grits and biscuits made my day already. Moms was putting it down upstairs. She hasn't had to leave this specially designed haven in over a few weeks. She invites her little friends over to play card games like Tonk or PittyPat and watch movies, just like slumber parties.

That's alright too. I know she enjoys her time upstairs and loves not having to go out and hustle for anything cuz her boy got that covered for her. I always will.

Today should be a good day, I already contacted Ivory and Cashmere and they' ll be ready at nine a.m. for me to take them to Hair Justice, a beauty salon on Fond du Lac Avenue. Roxanne and Sandra will be stylin' their dos.

Hopefully, they' ll be ready at one o' clock. I can drop them off to get their nails done, then to pick up some outfits and shoes from Blue' s place and let them get packed up. We' ll buy the bus tickets at the station tomorrow.

Right now I need to shit, let some water touch my ass, clean up a bit, get fresh, cop a crisp haircut and shave. My guy over at Gee' s Clippers will have me looking dapper.

LaQuanda' s party begins at nine, I'll make a guest appearance at around ten-thirty or twelve black folks time. I'd better get her a going away present. Nah, I'll give her five hundred dollars for her expenses.

Moving out of town ain't such a bad idea now that I think about it. A person can get too damn old here in this city and begin to feel like they can't go anywhere else and prosper.

I should make plans to make a move to another city somewhere like Atlanta, Miami or even Houston. I know I can make bread in any of those states. But I don't want to go alone.

I got a few connections down there and I'm sure the girls would like to go on an extended vacation like that.

I ain't a full-blooded pimp but I definitely got pimpin' ways. They can make that paper down there fo' sho'. The South is where its at for hustling. Bitches be throwin' that ass down there like Brett Favre of the Green Bay Packers throw his football missles. The only thing niggas gotta do is catch that ass if they can. Damn, just the thought of moving down there gets me hopeful.

A new start and a new beginning would be good for me. I've been in this city all my damn life and I want more than what I've been offered.

Snow Bunny Issues

Where the fuck is Precious?!

I've been calling and calling leaving messages on his phone to get in touch with me. I've made my decision about the escorting and truthfully I'm tired of forging and everything else. It was great while it lasted but I suppose it would be wise to move on now while I'm ahead.

Hustling like that was super easy for me because of who I am and how I look. I mean, how many stores and their personnel are *really* going to question me? I'm a rich white bitch plus, my appearance displays just that.

Who knows, I may even meet a rich guy who would want to marry me or a movie producer who'd want to make a dame like myself a movie star. Hell, a modeling agent would love to make me a supermodel. Conceited? A little.

Technically, I don't need to lift a finger of any kind to make any money due to my family's riches and my personal trust fund account. Nevertheless, I've always been attracted to the fast life and bad boys. Most people would literally kill to be in my high- heeled Jimmy Choo stilettos but they wouldn't have wanted to sport these bad babies while I was enduring the bullshit I had no choice but to endure growing up in my parents' home.

A Daddy's girl, I always was especially during the times he had begun to touch me in places that I now know weren't appropriate for a father to do.

When I was younger he would molest me by fondling and sucking my titties explaining that that was normal for a father to touch his daughter. My mother would be either asleep or away vacationing somewhere. She would never take me on her little trips to the Netherlands or Australia. Instead, I was left alone and scared with the thoughts of what might or would happen while left at the house with a sexual maniac.

The fondling lasted 'til I was almost twelve when other things began to happen. There were the times daddy would come into the bathroom while I was bathing to "help" wash me up. Even as a little girl, I expressed to him how very capable I was to do that myself but no, he persisted in helping me anyway if that's what you would call it. After watching me dry myself off, he would want to rub baby oil on my body and in doing so, he would get so turned on, I could see the imprint of his dick rising from his pajamas.

Before I was thirteen, he would make me touch him down there while he kissed me on the mouth.

Sneaking into bed with me in the middle of the night, he would push up against me and caress my body like a boyfriend would his girlfriend. Next thing I knew, he was probing his fingers into my pussy fingering me. The sad part is, I didn't know whether to like it or not. It felt good. My heart told me it was wrong and disgusting but my body would betray me.

A year later, daddy convinced me into giving him some head then he would give me some. That bullshit would happen at least three times a day like clockwork. When my delinquent ass mother was around she didn't notice shit, but I think deep down she already knew and stayed away just not to have to deal with it. The jerk and I would sneak around and tongue kiss each other behind her back, but remember, he always told me that that shit was normal all over the world. If it was so fucking normal, why did we have to sneak around like that?

At fifteen, he and I were having fully blown intercourse. He made certain that spermicidal jelly was used. He hated condoms. The sex would happen at least twice daily. Forever horny, I don't think he ever had sexual relations with mother anymore.

For me not telling anyone about us, he would reward me with expensive gifts from jewelry stores. Due to these sexual activities, my body developed more quickly than the other girls and boys would notice at school. When I did finally work up the courage to have a boyfriend, Daddy would try and act like he was fond of the lad knowing damn well he was jealous.

The boy's name was Alexander Cunningham. We went out for several months before he asked for sex. When the time did come for us to have relations he noticed that I wasn't a virgin. Getting me drunk one night, Alex asked me who was my first. Alcohol has the tendency to produce all sorts of truths out of you, and with drinking it, I accidentally blurted out who it was.

Boy oh boy, that changed shit between us instantaneously. Alex would no longer come over to my house, much to Daddy's delight. Alex even went a step further and told a social worker at our school what I had said. I had to speak with this woman about Alex's allegations and I denied them all.

How could I tell anyone? She must have known I was lying and made me watch some films pertaining to that subject. After watching those damn films, that's when it hit me that what had been happening was illegal and morally disgusting. Fathers didn't do what he did to me to their daughters everywhere. If they did, they were committing a crime. Looking at my jewelry collection for a teenager would make any grown woman cry profusely.

Well, all that was done in the dark and in secrecy eventually was bound to come to light. One night we were in my room fucking and mother walked in on us. I'll never forget that night. She screamed, cried and threw whatever she could get her hands on at us. Grabbing a hammer, I knew she was going to kill us but luckily a chambermaid had made the wise decision to call the police. Mother had to be sedated by the medics. Daddy was scared shitless when they were there because the police had questioned him about what was causing the commotion.

Any other time he was calm and collected but the look of death was on his face this time. So I blurted out the deal. I told them my mother had walked in on us having sex. The looks on the cops' faces were surreal. Daddy was arrested and I was taken to the hospital for examinations.

The doctors confirmed I had been having sex with my father once tests were ran on the sperm found in me. Mom was still under the influence of drugs and he was released on $500,000 bail. Instead of staying to face the consequences he fled the country. Leaving mom and I behind to have to deal with this shit, we both ended up on prescription drugs and in heavy counseling. Thru some investigation, I found out that the man who I thought was my father actually wasn' t.

To this day I visit a psychotherapist for the shit that happened to me during my childhood. And here people think I have it made because I'm rich and white but if only they knew the whole story they would feel differently.

I think this escort thing sounds ok though. I can travel expense free and make extra money doing it. I always thought about doing this especially after hearing how the girls who worked for a Hollywood madam would gross $40,000 a month escorting wealthy men. Hell, I should've been in the business a long time ago.

I suppose Precious expects for me to report to him about all my earnings though he made a point mentioning that I couldn't catch a forgery case for it.

With his mother being ill he could use a little helping out. It's not just one sided with he and I. We do for each other. I need to move out of state anyhow to begin anew. There' s nothing like a fresh start.

Hoe Acquisitions

The party was nice with everyone looking like they were having a good ol' time. The food was catered: barbequed chicken breasts and wings; homemade macaroni and cheese; a seven layered salad; black-eyed peas and yellow rice; gumbo; turkey dressing; mashed potatoes and gravy; green beans and corn; lasagna; catfish filets; cranberry sauce; stewed tomatoes; buttered croissants and wheat rolls was the menu. Her people spared no expense on the food obviously. Hell, they even had strawberry, chocolate chip and key lime cheesecake from the Cheesecake Factory for dessert. And what kind of black party is it without the honorary caramel cake?

LaQuanda has lost a little weight and she's looking damn good. Damn, I wanna tap that. The worst part about it all is I never got the chance to hit it more than twice. Dang. It's all to the good though, things happen for a reason.

I bid LaQuanda well and gave her my gift in an envelope and shook the spot.

Just getting off the phone with Kelly, she invited me to stop by. Maybe she's not interested in my suggestion. If not, I'll understand. I can't force a broad to do what they don't want to do.

I ain't a gorilla. That shit ain't cool no got damn way.

She came to the door dressed in a robe and her hair was in a bun. Kelly looked pretty without even really trying. We fixed ourselves cocktails and sat down by the mantelpiece. She looked like something was bothering her. Damn, did I do something wrong?

Anyway, after some conversation about everyday life she tells me that she's down for the program and all I have to do is be there for her whenever she needs me. I do that already so this should be easy as rolling a big black shiny ball down the lane to knock down the redneck pins.

Now a phone call needs to be placed, some papers faxed and signed and she can get started as soon as this week. Man, I'll have three beautiful women working for me. This venture could prove to be fun provided everything goes according to plan.

I need to put some money away for a coupla of things. Hard times can fall down at any given time without warning.

Loc might need some help with attorney fees the way shit is happenin' out here in these streets. That nigga lived life to the fullest every day as if there was no tomorrow. Vacationing to the islands and overseas; fifty thousand dollar shopping sprees; boat cruises; major event kickin' it to the boxing matches in Vegas; the Source award shows; music award shows; the Essence music festivals and the Superbowls.

Anything happening he was guaranteed to be there. I suppose living the life he was living it' d be wise to live it up because one day all that splurging could come to an end for a playa when least expected. You either gotta prepare for death or the penitentiary if you're not wise enough to get out while the getting was good.

High Class Whorin'

It'll be working for the Florida agency this month, then next month the other one in Hollywood. My first assignment is in Chicago, which is good because I can drive over and afterwards do some shopping.

The gentleman I'm scheduled to meet is an investment banker, never married, middle aged and his name is Brock. We're scheduled to meet at the Hyatt in downtown Chicago.

For four hours of my time I'll be compensated $4000. The agency gets their forty percent off the top and I'll expect this man to know he is expected to tip me generously. I may have some fun while I'm at it. For festivities, we'll be going to a jazz spot, dinner at an exclusive restaurant, and back to the hotel.

I'll wear my slinky black knit dress, black Louis Vuitton boots with the matching Louis Vuitton Theda handbag. For my personal overnight stay I'll pack some Moschino jeans, a pink cashmere sweater and a few toiletries.

I'm relieved to know this agency takes every precaution to ensure the validity of their clients. All the information is kept strictly confidential and their clients are thoroughly screened to verify who they say they are. There are crazy fools out there and I'm not even trying to be in any ill trouble on account of some trick.

Oh well, it's time for me to get ready for my "new" job. I have to bathe and set my hair. My pedicure and manicure was taken care of earlier today.

Precious offered to go with me but something else came up. He wanted to do some shopping for his house. I do know that if we don't get serious with each other then I'll have no choice but to move on. Out of state preferably. Surely he doesn't think that I haven't grown to have feelings for him by this time.

Hmph, ol' father dear would be seriously incensed if he knew what's been happening with me, but I wonder if he would even really care. I need to call my psychotherapist next week.

Two hours later …

Brock was a nice looking gentleman and very well dressed in his Armani suit. The shoes he wore were Prada. His hair was stylishly cropped cut and sandy brown in color. His eyes were light green and he had dimples when he smiled showing super straight white teeth.

Damn, I could get used to this lifestyle. We're on our way to the jazz function and I can tell he appreciates my demure sophistication. I do wonder where we'll be dining for dinner. I dine at the most posh establishments so it'll be interesting to see his choice for us.

The jazz concert and supper should last for at least three hours then he'll have just one hour left to spend time with me. He compensated me in cash and the agency received their cut by credit card.

We had supper at a fancy seafood place the food was exceptional. I'm really having a nice time with him. Thus far, he's been the perfect gentleman. High-class money puts you around high-class people with high-class tastes.

Surprisingly, sex wasn't the only issue with Brock. He wanted to talk and get to know me. I suppose being able to buy all the pussy in any part of the world is nothing to him by now. Having made it back to the hotel our evening ended with him rubbing my feet.

I wasn't expecting anything like that at all. Imagine getting paid nicely for socialization. He wanted to spend more time with me but rules are rules and I didn't want to mess up my first day on the job. Nevertheless, he tipped an extra thousand dollars.

I made thirty-four hundred dollars total. Cool.

I hope he liked me enough to want to set up another date when he comes into town with the agency. There's no telling what he's willing to do for a woman.

I'll get another room on a different floor and go sightseeing after I change into something more comfortable. Shopping on the Magnificent Mile tomorrow seems like a great plan. Then I'll come back to the room to unwind and relax.

On Point

Meanwhile back in Milwaukee, Precious was putting the finishing touches on his place while all of the girls were off working.

Up north at a strip club where Ivory and Cashmere were working it was going pretty slow for the past two days but was sure to pick up later in the week. In order to make any type of money tricks would have to be pulled.

If a gal could pull five good dates or more she would be sure to make a thousand off of fucking. The club is strictly for campaigning. Men can see what a woman has to offer before he goes home. He can fantasize fondling, licking and sticking whoever was his favorite girl of the night.

Ivory was able to pull a date out the club, she got paid two hundred from the mark.

Cashmere stayed outside the room to give them privacy and to keep watch for someone she herself could pull. The trick Ivory got was an older white man who visited the club frequently in hopes of finding a young black girl to satisfy his yearnings.

Normally, a two girl private show would entail some freaky shit plus the man getting got for whatever money, jewelry or credit cards he had if the girls were thieves. Some tricks get caught out there slippin'.

Thirsty Desires

Cashmere saw someone cruising past the hotel back and forth looking at her. She noticed the man was rollin' a late model Benz. He finally parked his car and stood outside his car door waiting for her to come down to talk to him. For one reason or another, she didn't feel up to walking down to him. He would have to come to her if he wanted some business. That way, she didn't commit solicitation, which could land her in jail and prostitution fines.

The girls already know to allow the man to proposition and not to touch the money directly from their hands but to take it from a table. It's getting trickier and trickier to hoe nowadays.

On Thursday, work picked up heavily for the two girls and both were fairly busy throughout the night and early morning. Between Monday and Wednesday they both only netted about five hundred together. Thursday thru Saturday the girls each pulled in about a thousand a piece and with that coupled with the weekly check, they each made roughly close to fifteen hundred for that week.

After two weeks up north of working at the club and side hustling they should be checkin' in about five thousand plus to Precious.

The marks up north were relatively safe. The town was small and a lot of hunting goes on up there around wintertime. The hunting season was coming up in a few weeks, so the girls took it upon themselves to book work for those two weeks much to the owner Fancy' s, delight. Fancy hadn't seen such nice looking black girls in quite some time. Ivory and Cashmere were exceptionally beautiful and sure to attract more business.

It's no secret that the homely looking white girls at the club were jealous of all the attention the sisters were getting so that's when the player hatin' began.

First, it was drinks being spilled in the girl's area. Ivory and Cashmere noticed but didn't think too much of it. Then, the girls noticed that their personal hygiene stuff was being tampered with. Baby wipes were gone too quickly, smell good perfumes were missing and then outfits were misplaced. So being the smooth gals that they are they opted to keep their shit on lockdown in lockers. Game was peeped and the gals kept their eyes wide open.

One white girl at the club, Snow, pulled Cash to the side and hipped her to the bullshit jumping off. Snow was the type of hoe that was built like a black girl and from the hood.

Her pimp daddy was a nigga who went by the name Shema, from the gutters of Brown Street. His mother was known for strollin' the blocks and his biological pops was a deadbeat from Chicago.

Neither his mother nor grandparents raised Shema. The streets raised him and he graduated from the school of hardknocks. He was a dirty little nigga comin' up. Bustin' fools up side the head was his trademark.

Years down the line he learned how to sell fake product made of drywall, baking soda and boric acid. The fiends he sold that shit to would get sick but they were also scared of him. Word spread through the alleys not to cop shit from him cause it just wasn't right.

Eventually, an old player named Big Black pulled the scraggly kid by his collar and offered him a job running shit on a bike from one location in the neighborhood to another. Black looked out for the kid and bought him fresh gear and shoes. An allowance of a hundred dollars a week was also allotted to him.

Soon enough peeps began to look differently at Shema while he was gaining a rep of respect. Girls that shunned his dirty little ass were noticing him now. Being that he didn't have a mother figure in his life he didn't quite know how to treat girls. Whenever he got with a girl he was extremely quiet but if the girl ever showed signs of getting ready to leave him, he would smack her around.

It ain't a secret that the young buck needed some hood anger management. Strange thing was, when he was around his boys he was all thug but when alone he was a totally different character. Yep, he's the type that had to have his henchmen around him in order to feel important. All that was a front to make a long story short.

If some of the girls he fucked with had brothers and cousins that played no games, he didn't lay a hand on them, but if she didn' t, he would beat the dog shit out of her to only buy her gifts to make up for his actions. Some girls were g' d for that bullshit of getting their asses thoroughly kicked physically. Mentally, some of the girls he dealt with had some serious self-esteem issues but some weren't totally screwed up in the head.

As the years passed, Shema became the top man in the game shelling out crazy product- marijuana, cocaine, crack and x. His squad of goons would travel down south to Texas to get fresh and bring back the goods for quick distribution. It didn't take long for him to reach millionaire status.

The latest bitch he was with, Isis, had minks and leather jackets of many colors with matching shoes and boots to match. Purses were unlimited and the girl's wardrobe was fit for the stars. Word is she didn't mind getting pummeled around late nights after Shema came in from drinking and clubbin'. She was in it for the material wealth and recognition. Fuck the respect.

Putting his key in the door one night, Shema staggered in the house and belted out, "Baby, where you at?"

When there was no answer he got agitated. So he hollered out again. Still when there was no answer he made his way to the bedroom to see his girl asleep with head phones on. For one reason or another that irritated the hell outta him and he pulled the covers from the bed.

She was only wearing panties and feeling the night air she woke up to see him standing over her with his dick in his hand. Taking off the headset, she rubbed her eyes and asked what the hell was wrong with him.

"Bitch, wake up and put this dick in your mouth," he retorted.

"Baby, I'm tired and it's four o' clock in the morning," she whimpered after looking at the clock on the nightstand.

"So what your telling me is, you want me to just stand here with my dick in my hand while you go back to sleep huh?"

"No, I guess not," she sass mouthed to him.

"Bitch, I run this shit and I run you too so I strongly advise you to stand up to my plate and handle your business or else I'mma have to put these beaters on you and frankly I ain't in the mood to be kickin' you in your ass right now," he told her. "I rescued yo punk ass from nothing so you need to be real quick to show me some muthafuckin' appreciation ' round this here and handle your duties," he growled.

At the mere threat of violence from him, she raised up and slobbered on his dick knowing that if she resisted any more or longer she could end up with a fat lip, bloody nose, a closed eye or all of the above. She never called the pigs to press charges on him whenever he put his foot up her ass cause she knew that would be the end of her material easy livelihood that she became accustomed to.

She was from the hood too and her mother was lost out in the world. Her father didn't exist. Growing up, she had to make do with living with swarms of roaches and rodents. Sleeping on dirty shabby mattresses, its not like she had much to look forward to everyday.

During her school days she was the kid that got teased because of the old clothes she wore. No one bothered to comb her hair or help make her presentable. One day, she vowed to herself to catch a man who would take care of her and show her a better life.

She met Shema at a neighborhood bar called Tap One down on Locust Street. When she saw him she thought he was kind of cute with his oddly shaped head. She imagined that he was dropped or fell out of the crib or something when he was little.

At eye contact she was attracted to this man she heard of thru the grapevine but looking into his eyes she felt a bit of compassion for him. She heard the rumors and believed that with showing and giving him good loving like he never had it before that she could tame the inner beast in him.

He on the other hand, saw her gazing him down seeing a doe he could control and manipulate. Shema was a predator and green women were his prey. He nodded for her to come over to where he was sitting. Eventually the weeks passed and she was smitten with his bad boy persona. All he needed for her *not* to do was leave him. He abhorred the idea of being alone. She became his wifey while he pimped part-time and sold drugs.

She believed that Shema wasn't all that rotten. Thus, taking a slappin' around and the occasional punch was a small price to pay to be able to floss in the streets with her furs and expensive gear. On the days she had a black eye she wore her Gucci shades. When her lip was fat she iced it and stayed in the house. Days when her body ached from fighting with Shema, she popped pain pills and carried on like an obedient soldier. Deep down she hoped one day that Shema would realize what he did to her in his drunken stupors was wrong and would change. As of yet, that day hadn't appeared and it probably never would. She couldn't help but to keep hope alive.

Snow was his bottom hoe who brought in lots of money and drug customers. He didn't dare lay a hand on her because for one, she was white and a black man hitting a white woman in Wisconsin was asking for jail time off top. Snow's addict buddies brought him thousands a month and to fuck up an arrangement like that wouldn't be beneficial to the cause.

Snow at the least brought him twenty-five to three thousand a week from whoring alone. That's far more money any one broad in two weeks ever brought to him. The drug customers were an extra two g's easily.

His main broad didn't have to worry about havin' to go out in the field to bring him any money back home. He just wanted someone to be there at the house at all times waiting on him to come in. Shema felt secure knowing someone was at home just for his pleasure.

His woman, Isis, on the other hand was getting fed up with his bullshit and the abuse. She had love for Shema but the garbage was wearing her thinner and thinner.

It got to the point that whenever he came into the house her stomach would tie in knots with the worries of whether or not he had been drinking or if he had a good day.

As of late though, she had been beginning to wonder what life could be like without all the hassles. Her thoughts took in consideration of the material comfort she lived daily.

Sooner or later a great decision would have to be made. Whose to say that staying wouldn't eventually cost her her life?

Happy Hoes Get More Money

The girls oughta be back pretty soon and a nigga cain't wait to check that grip. I already bought them some fur coats at the sale that was held down by Mitchell airport. I'll present the coats to them a week after their return.

For Ivory, a white fox jacket with the matching fur headband and muffle was chosen. For Cashmere, a full-length black ranch mink was chosen also with a matching fur headband.

These coats should show them how much I appreciate them and in return, they'll appreciate me as well and bring me even more spinach. Gotta keep the hoes happy. I'll have to find some matching bags for them to wear with the furs.

Another plan in motion is to send them down to New Orleans for the Mardi Gras festival. Onyx was planning on going down there with all his girls and he said he could take my babes with his squad while I handled the home front. That's good lookin'.

I like to think it's important to tell folks how you feel about them before its too late. El is like a big brother to me and I really appreciate now he always looked out for me whenever I needed him. Good friends are hard to find and keeping a good friend can be even harder.

He asked me along on the trip with him but someone needs to stay here to watch over our mothers.

"Say dog, why don't you roll down to the N.O. with me and bring your girls down to make some money," Onyx asked. "I know for a fact that they could cop a few thousand during the festival, tricks will be everywhere," he told Precious. "I took a few girls last year and we stayed for three weeks straight. We came home with ten thousand dollars easy."

I've been to Mardi Gras twice before and it's the same old thing: hoes, hoes, hoes, and more hoes. Having fun out of town is his thang. El gets a thrill from pleasure and money.

The money the girls make for me helps and Kelly has been doing wonderfully with the escort agencies. Kelly goes on call at least four times a week. Why it is white women get paid far more money than black women, I'll never understand. For now, she'll be the bottom. The rules of the game are the rules of the game. One rule being that whoever pulls in the most change is the one who gets the most favoritism. But hey, every pimp should have at least one bad ass looking white hustlin' whore in the stable.

To date I have accumulated well over twenty-five thousand. With half of it put away for safekeeping, I spent the other half on home repairs, life insurance policies, a bracelet for Kelly and clothes for the girls. As a businessman, I figured I better get life insurance policies on the girls too. Those policies can come in handy. I bought $250,000 policies on Ivory, Cashmere, and Kelly. The only beneficiary on those policies was I. I paid the schedules with the money they gave me.

I don't plan on managing them forever anyhow, but enough to accomplish the things I set out to do. The girls must eventually establish themselves and make their own way, but in the meantime, as long as their willing to give me hoe money I'm going to accept it with open hands. I do want them to go to school, save some money and have something to fall back on eventually. A hoe especially a good-looking hoe can only hoe for so long.

A lot of pimps are afraid of smart hoes. A smart whore will learn the craft of making money and put it away eventually investing in her future. It's funny to me how a woman could be in the game for years and have nothing to show for it. I worry just a little for them. Thugs have feelings too.

My intentions have for the most part been good, and when you do good, its returned to you tenfold. Do evil shit and it will also be turned to you twenty-fold. Give me the good return any day.

In late January, it was time to prepare the girls for New Orleans. They were treated to full body massages, hair dos, hand and feet treatments and dinners. Blue helped me out with new outfits and shoes for this trip of two weeks. All in all, both of them got at least ten new fits and shoes.

They love me and I love them. Without them I wouldn't be able to do what I've been doing. I have no problem treating my ladies to spa and beauty treatments and classy dinners, they deserve it.

El doesn't pamper his girls like I pamper mine. El was well known in the streets of Milwaukee due to his pimping. And as far as I know, he was respected yet envied by the other pimps as well. Onyx was famous for his cars, jewelry and his style. With his wavy hair and slim build, the women would clamor for his attention. He was considered a pretty playa. His appearance was flawless. Girls would want to be down with El so bad that when he was in Chicago on the strip, he could park his car and leave the windows cracked and go to a mall for an hour or two. Upon returning, piles of confetti of the legal tender persuasion would be on the front seats and floor of his car. He had me help him count the loot and in one night we counted nine thousand plus dollars in trick money.

A nigga gotta have one hell of a reputation to have hoes hustlin' the streets of Chicago that's not even in his stable tossin' they pimps money in his car. El was chosen so hard that he had to turn some girls away even though they chose him.

Naturally, pimps felt snubbed that some prettyboy could just up and command the baddest of hoes off his looks alone. But that wasn't the case totally. When Onyx pimped, he pimped callously.

Nevertheless, drama was sure to ensue.

For history purposes, a family of thugs and pimps, known as the Freports, jumped him on. The Freports were well known for being involved in both the drug and pimp trade. All the men in the family were groomed for hustlin' tax-exempt money.

There's no doubt that they would have their girls at every major event from the football Classics to the Black Expos to the boxing events in Nevada and Atlantic City. Those gorillas rolled Jags and Beamers.

Their hoes clocked major chips. Then again, they had no choice either because if they didn't bring in what they were supposed to then they could look forward to getting dealt with.

Troubles Brewing

For one reason or another, I was quite concerned about his leaving on this trip down South. Rumors were in the streets that something ugly was bound to happen down there that would rock the city. For weeks, no one had a clue as to what exactly was to happen. El knew there was animosity against him, yet he didn't pay it any mind, he stayed on his grind.

Two weeks before the festival, everyone hopped a plane down there and rented motel rooms not to far from the strip clubs the Roxbury and She-s for He-s. There were about ten girls in total with him and he had to rent six rooms, two girls to a room.

The girls didn't have to begin their work at the clubs until the evening but they had to put their stunting down during the day. Some gals did so well on the tracks they didn't have to work at the clubs. A couple of his girls would make about two thousand a day and the quota was one thousand. With so many tourists and visitors from all over the States it was relatively simple to make that kind of change in a day.

Before they left, El had a shopping plastic bag full of condoms, spermicidal jelly, and lubricating jelly for the girls to use. Preparation was essential when it came to the pursuit of loot. At the end of the first week he told me all his hoes had net close to fifteen thousand for that week and mine had clocked in about five stacks.

Near the end of the two-week period he had close to nineteen grand while my broads net figure was close to nine grand. That's a lot of pussy selling, standing on toes, dick slobbin', ass lickin' and fuckin'.

I instructed my ladies, cuz that's what they *really* are, to wire me eight grand, take a cab to the airport and come on home. They all arrived that Monday afternoon in Milwaukee safe and in one piece.

El decided to stay down for at least another week. I asked him to wire his bread to me to put up but he said he had it all in a safe spot. It wasn't for me to sweat him ' bout his grip but I had a funny feeling about him down there like a sitting duck.

Damn near every pimp in the game was in New Orleans. Known for tossing their baddest bitches on another pimp to get in the biz. That's what happened with El.

As the story was told, a hoe from the Southside of Chicago sweated El vigorously. Being a sucka for mo' money he allowed her to work for him.

Now see in the pimp game, when a hoe chooses another pimp to pander her, the original pimp is called upon to smooth the shit over. Well that's what was supposed to happen. The broad called herself Isis and was able to peep the money El had accumulated. Upon that view, she went back to her original daddy to put the bug in his ear. The happenings after that brought the downfall.

One night all the girls were out working and a group of cats went to El's room but El wasn't aware that those niggas were out to set him up for the oke-doke. El knew some of the marks from pimp parties thus, he fell off his square thinking everything was all cool and dandy. Tooting cocaine and drinking two hours more or less later, these same cats murdered El.

Their first step of torture was roughing him up and when that didn't work, hot cooking grease from the microwave in the room was poured down his lap. The mission of torture was to find his money but that was thwarted when the police were called to the sounds of bloodcurdling screams and a gunshot. The money was stashed one of the rooms. Which one, no one knows. Everyone had to check out after that bullshit went down.

Only El will ever know who did him in but one day I will find out just who those muthafuckas were and handle that business myself. In essence, he was murdered for something ... sheer jealously and hatred. The remaining girls of his called me and I instructed them to bail the fuck outta dodge asap. All but two of them came back home. I think the two that went awol both found the money and went their own way or the other pimps kidnapped them. I never heard from them again after all that madness went down. Rumor has it that the broads went to Texas and set up shop there. I plan to find them hoes too.

I lost my best friend, my confidante and my brother. I was so hurt, confused and devastated my life was at a stand still for weeks. I couldn't sleep well, eat, drink or drive straight. I was mourning the death of the only true friend I had. I loved El.

His mother had lost a lot of weight and her appearance had deteriorated due to the devastating blow of losing her only child to the streetlife. She was taking it hard drinking hard liquor from sun up to sun down. I have never witnessed her off the track of business. El was the love of her life, her lifeline, the only sure thing she had and he was scandalously ripped from her. She eventually had to move in with us for a while. So it was on me to watch over the houses and maintain sanity while helping to watch over my second mother. My process of mourning was halted and I vow to avenge the death of my brother.

After two weeks, investigators from neither New Orleans nor Milwaukee had any solid leads that would stick. Just speculation and that meant nothing. Hard evidence was needed and no one was talking. That's one code of the streets, when shit happens, no one is supposed know shit about shit. His mother had to make the decision to either have the funeral in Milwaukee or out of state. She chose the latter. With that decision she also liquidated her assets and said her goodbyes to us as well. We fully understood how and why she did. Her houses were sold and now my mom Phyllis has not only lost a second son but her best friend as well too.

El's remaining girls decided to keep on working for me at this point. I had a stable of eight and I wasn't quite sure if I could handle it but for the memory of my brother, I was going to put it down. I immediately bought another house, fixed it up and had the girls living there. It was another duplex with a total of six bedrooms. Therefore I had to renovate the basement to install an additional toilet. That arrangement worked out well until I was able to buy yet another house. I then split all the girls up to four to a house and I had even bought two cars for them to get around in.

These gals were bred for ho' ing. Forever on the paper chase. Soon enough, I had no choice but to buy them all lovely gifts of appreciation. Every month, I was seeing close to sixty-five grand a month. I was havin' way more money than I could ever dream of havin'. They deserve the best of everything I can give them. Kelly was still doing her thang and a fly entrepreneur like myself was catching at least twenty stacks from her alone per week.

They all didn't know it yet, but I was planning a month long cruise vacation for all of us to Jamaica, the Virgin Islands, and the Bahamas. I surprised the girls with the news and the tickets. I swear, I never heard so much damn squealing and hackling before in my life. During the expedition, we saw the beautiful Jamaican islands and marveled at the native peoples. We all snorkeled damn near everyday plus scuba dived. I went all out for them; they deserved the best treatment. I just can't take anyone for granted who take chances for me like they do.

Kelly went on a vacation of her own to Canada to see some relatives. Something strange is going on with her plus her appearance isn't like it used to be. Maybe there' s a sickness or something going on in her family that she hasn't bothered to relay to me. Whatever the situation is I hope she snaps out of it. I plan to have a sit down with her about all the happenings over a nice dinner.

I need to catch up with people I haven't spoken with in a long while. With all the dramas unfolding I just haven't had the time. Female companionship has basically been like a faraway thought. Jane't will have to get a phone call from me soon. I'm just about ready to settle down with someone anyhow.

Drugs And Death

Out on a date with a rock star, Kelly was introduced to the drugs heroin and x. After the first few tries with the drugs she became disoriented and addicted. She liked the feelings.

Doing heroin will have a person completely out of their character. That first hit orbits a person to cloud eleven. The infamous noddin' syndrome. X on the other hand will get a person ready for explosive sex with just about anyone. If a person has never had sex in the ass before due to the fear of pain it was obsolete after doing some x. That drug makes people act out like they are bonafide porn stars.

Soon thereafter, Kelly was buying the dope in ounces to use in the privacy of her home. At first she was snorting the drug on her social engagements. Shortly after becoming addicted, she began to shoot it up her veins to achieve that seemingly more ultimate high. A gorilla was on her back.

Question now was would she be able to shake it? Precious saw some of the changes in her but just discredited it to a death or illness in the family. She hadn't told him of any issues she was having that affected her. He had no inkling she was an addict under drugstress.

The rock star that turned her out on the drugs didn't have to go through the agency anymore to hook up with Kelly. She had gone against he rules and given the rocker her personal phone numbers to contact her and she hung out with him more often than not, out in Hollywood. Before too long, she was heavily dating this punk. The tabloid magazines portrayed them as being lovers having photographed them. The escort agency fired her upon learning of that information. Their escorts were to be discreet and not being that, Kelly wasn't obviously living up to her obligations needing to be dismissed.

Precious was having so much money he didn't miss the change from her at all yet he still cherished their friendship. Not long after he acquired his vast stable, she had made the conscious decision to wean herself from him preparing to move on to seemingly bigger, better things. Over the course of a year she'd given him well over two hundred grand. At that point she felt she had done all she was going to do for him.

All she ever got out of the deal was a twenty carat bracelet, five carat yellow diamond earrings, a couple of furs and heartache. The material possessions she already had access to. She was already a rich bitch.

The one thing she ultimately needed and yearned to have access to is what Precious wouldn't give to her …his heart. He made it his business to remain distant to any love connections that he wasn't feeling.

She needed someone to talk to about her past. She needed someone to love her unconditionally. Someone she could count on when she was down. Someone to believe in her and what she had to offer to a union, the real shit. Someone to rub her shoulders to show her that everything would surely be all gravy. Someone she could trust explicitly with her heart. Someone to love, who in return would love her back as strongly as she loved. Life was a living nightmare for her.

Even though she had mad access to money and anything a woman could ever want, she still wasn't fulfilled and happy. The incestual abuse she suffered as a child was catching up to her emotionally and mentally. She never confronted the man she knew as her father about his misdeeds. Her mother blocked the whole episode out of her own mind. Her racist grandparents were long dead and buried. Her other relatives were folks she hardly knew. So in essence, whom did she really have on her team? Who could she have had? Damn, whom could she count on? All those questions permeated her mental on the daily.

She was weary. Tired of the games people played with her; tired of the people she grew to love misusing her for their own greedy gains; tired of being disappointed in herself for allowing the bullshit to happen in the first place; tired of being let down and run over; tired of being taken for granted and truly unappreciated.

The only relief she got from all the despair and internal pain was thru the use of the drugs. The drugs were her safe haven from the outside world, just after using them she felt invincible and lovable ...u ntil the high left. Then she wouldn't feel so damn good. Her body would be in pain plus, her body would wretch from the violent regurgitating sessions. Her head would pound like an anvil against a concrete block. Withdrawal was a muthafucka when it came to fucking with smack.

Her once beautiful looks had left her; even sags were underneath her once vibrant green eyes. She looked like a stoner. Lost. Her once healthy head of hair lost its bountiful luster and sheen. The bitch could have been in those hair commercials. Her body was withering away slowly because she rarely had an appetite for food. As time continued the sores from where she stuck the needles turned into abscesses. Basically, she didn't give a flying fuck about herself anymore. She was ready to die to escape the miseries that haunted.

Once she got hold of the drugs she considered essential to her well-being, everything would be better she thought. She could float off into heaven for a little while at the least. Picking up an expensive sterling silver Oneida spoon that was laying on her Brazilian imported nightstand, she carefully poured some powdered uncut heroin into its groove.

She believed she could handle a small pure uncut amount of the lethal drug. Kelly had already found a vein on the inside of her thigh so she hit it a couple of times with her hand and inserted the needle into her leg pushing the instrument necessarily far enough to dispense the drug into her bloodstream. At first she didn't feel anything but she also knew that given a few seconds she would. She saw stars and even the moon, euphoria. She didn't just see heaven anymore ...her soul went to it. The most beautiful thing she ever saw and felt.

Missing In Action

Upon returning from our vacation I noticed I hadn't yet heard anything from Kelly so I called her place to only get her voicemail.

"Hey Kelly, this is P and I've been trying to contact you for the past couple of days baby and you haven't returned any of my calls. So either you need to call me or I'll take a trip over there to see about you girl."

After leaving numerous messages for the past two days I began to worry that things just weren't right. I even stopped by the apartment building a couple of times. Finally, I reported to the doorman my suspicions and he too also said he hasn't seen or heard anything from Kelly either.

"Say man, I'm getting concerned about Kelly because I haven't heard from her and I normally do before it's a whole two days, have you seen her?" Precious asked the doorman Ralph.

"I can't say that I have and you know I'm always working these doors. She hasn't had any visitors for the longest cause she's been gone out of town plus, she has a mailbox full of mail still," he relayed to Precious.

"I think we should act like private investigators and see what's happenin' up there, I got a sick feeling to my stomach," Precious told Ralph.

We decided to go to her apartment just to check it out. We weren't even prepared for what we were about to encounter.

First, there was a peculiar odor in the house. It smelled like someone had taken a couple of steaks from their wrappers and neglected to take the garbage out. Pure shit. Then, we noticed that the apartment was a bit untidy; it looked as if it hadn't been cleaned in weeks and I know that to be unlike Kelly, she was such a neat freak.

As we walked into the bathroom we found piles of clothing layin' all over the place. When we ventured towards the bedroom, the odor became stronger and more pungent. I knew then that what we would find on the other side of her bedroom door would throw us into shock and disbelief. Opening the door cautiously, we found lying nude on the bed, Kelly. Her legs were hanging off of the foot of the bed. Her eyes were open and some of her body had turned blue and black. I noticed patches of dried snot on the cream duvet cover and under her nostrils. The foul odor apparently was from the defecation she had to have expelled as she was overdosing. Flies were flying around the crib like vultures, mad as hell cuz they were rudely interrupted.

How the muthafuckas got in the apartment was a mystery to me. The nasty fuckers were like hound dogs attracted to the death and decay.

The doorman called the cops while I did some more investigating on my own. I noticed down by her thigh there was a protruding needle. I have never known Kelly to entertain any type of drug yet I searched around the room for more clues. On the nightstand, I peeped a spoon with a dried up residue in it and a lighter was lying there right beside. I knew then that Kelly had overdosed on heroin.

I wondered if there was more drugs nearby, so I went looking for her purse. I found it in the living room under the papers. I found inside her Mizhani bag, a small vial containing some powder and another disposable needle. Her wallet still had all her credit cards, receipts, and identification in it. There was also close to two grand in the wallet. I held onto her identification and the money.

The receipts showed some purchases she had made in cash while she was in Chicago. I needed to find out who the fuck it was that she was with, when she was with they punk asses and what the hell they were doing that could have made her want to get turned out on drugs. Someone had turned her out.

Damn, did she really know what the fuck she was doing? The cops and detectives arrived within ten minutes and had questioned the doorman and myself, and then police photographers came and took pictures. They ruled in favor of drug overdose. Well, actually I already knew but a nigga had to play dumb cuz the pigs would have thought I was her dealer just by the color of my skin.

I didn't know too much about her family, so I called some numbers that were in her Palm Pilot. Before I left the apartment I grabbed a picture she and I had taken in Chicago, I was going to put it in a frame. I wonder if she even knew that I had grown fond of and cared for her. I wonder if she knew that if she needed help I would have been there for her whenever she needed me? I knew I didn't give her the time she would have liked to have from me. Hell, I'm a hustler. I guess I'll never know what she knew. Damn. A nigga's emotions clouded up the eye ducts. I wish I could have …coulda, woulda, shoulda. *DAMN*.

Bullshit Is Nothin'

Spring was only a day away, the time for fresh starts and newer beginnings. My ladies were still doing well in their chosen professions and I was still netting over fifty grand a month. And I had saved a nice amount, plus what I had stored in the safe deposit boxes including my investments, so I was comfortable enough to chill out for the next five years.

I had brought more property and was collecting rent from the tenants on rent assistance. Low and behold I never thought I would get a tenant like the one who called about the ad in the newspaper. I wanted to meet this seemingly intelligent young lady for an interview. Her voice sounded familiar but I wasn't quite sure who she was.

"Hello, my name is Jane't and I'm calling in regards to the newspaper ad that's in the Sunday paper. I don't have any children and I believe your choice in picking me, as your new tenant would be your best choice ever. I would appreciate a return phone call," she left on the voicemail.

Right then, I knew it wasn't anyone other than Jane't. I knew immediately that she was going to be my new tenant at this house I had bought and renovated over on Villard Avenue.

The house was a single family with two bedrooms, one and a half bathroom, living, dining, and kitchen along with a finished basement structure. I originally wanted to charge seven hundred for rent but since Jane't didn't have any crumb snatchers, she was only approved for five fifty thru the program. I didn't have a problem with that, good tenants are hard to find and I knew she would be a responsible one. She was just as surprised to see me also and I had to apologize to her for not keeping in touch with her.

The forces that be work in mysterious ways. We were reintroduced into each other' s lives.

At the time come to find out, she had been going out with a mark named James. The mark was claiming he was originally from down south somewhere but had been living in Milwaukee for over five years.

In my world, if you move anywhere and have been living there for three or more years, you're from the state where you have been living. She had expressed to me the problems she was having in their relationship. James had been cheating on her since the beginning of their relationship plus he wasn't satisfying her mentally, physically or monetarily.

I wondered why she chose to stay with the busta and just came out and asked. Her answer was because she was lonely. Boy o' boy, the thangs a woman would accept from a man befuddles me. And I can admit, I'm a man who at times has been on some extra shit. Foul shit.

I gave her the advice to break it off for a trial period and re- evaluate her options. Secretly, I wanted to be a part of her life again. This girl still got it going on and I'm ready to get with a winner and make some things happen. I know she still dug me too, hell, it was written all over her face.

Her breaking up with James wasn't too easy after all. Once she had told him of her plans to sever their relationship, he began to act crazy even to the point of stalking her. Wherever she went, he was there: grocery store, the laundromat, gas station, even the clubs. This nigga was layin' in the cut.

Whenever she was on the phone, he would call her at the most inopportune times. This James character was becoming a real pest to her and me. I was getting sick and tired of hearing ' bout the bullshit. There are ways of ridding the world of pests. Some men can't handle being men, therefore they resort to stupid shit like that bullshit was going to change anything for the better. Unbeknownst to me the situation was going to get worse.

One morning, I had left her house and I noticed someone was parked down a house or two just staring at a player. Somebody was watching me. I felt it. Since it was early, I didn't think much of it so I went on about my day. Apparently, that same chump I saw was James. Not too long after my departure, he had gone over to the house to try to talk to Jane't and instead of doing only that, he took it upon himself to jump on her.

He had beaten her up so badly, she had to go to the hospital for treatment of the open wounds, bruises and broken bones. The asshole even went so far as to threaten to kill her and commit suicide if they weren't going to be together. His bitch ass even pistol- whipped her.

I didn't find all this out until the day after it happened. James had also robbed her of her jewelry, furs, money and high tech shit. I bet my bottom dolla' the mark didn't pay a dime for any of it either. I have no respect for men that feel they can use women as their personal punching bags and then expect for those women to forgive and forget what they had done.

Well Jane't was a smarter one, she had decided to press charges against the crazy fool and hopefully he' ll be put away for a long time. If the fake ass justice system don't put him away for a while then I'll handle the justice she needs. It takes nothing for me to make a phone call to my nigga Scar. He has a sick obsession with torturing fools and gnawing on their flesh. He doesn't come out until dark and to have him tell it, he's a modern age vampire. Niggas in the joint don't care too much for men who hurt women and children anyway, yet along the sorry sons of bitches who' d rob a woman too.

Little does he know he just made the opening better for a real man to step up to the shattered plate and make everything far better than what it ever was. He' ll suffer his consequences eventually.

That's on my word.

I went and stayed with her because she needed company. The dumb ass nigga should have stepped to me instead and his ass woulda been found stankin' somewhere. But no, he had to step to a defenseless woman. Coward. She kept a gun, but it wasn't at the house during that incident.

I can only imagine the outcome if it *was* there and she was able to get to it.

Jane't had called me. "Hey Precious, I really want to thank you for staying with me the other night because I needed company like yours. I filed the charges and even a restraining order but the district attorney already told me that James would most likely only receive probation for what he did."

"Do you want me to handle this situation since the white man' s system ain't trying to do shit about it?"

"Well, I already know that what goes around comes around and if I were to sic you and your peeps on him, that my full blessings would be blocked and I need all the blessings I can get yanno," she said.

Damn. That shocked the shit out of me. What happened to good old revenge? I told her that it *would* be a blessing for me to have ol' boy handled to the fullest. Punk niggas like that don't have the proper organs to evolve the dick and balls to step to another man like that. But hearing that revelation from Jane't let me know already that she was a winner in this game of life.

Classy. Yet, there was something incredibly calculating to how she said it. She ain't telling me something. I gotta figure it out but she ain't gonna make it easy. She was way to serene with all the bullshit that went down. Way to level-headed. The shit was damn near eerie.

The mark didn't get charged with the armed robbery or the attempted murder. His bitch ass got off with aggravated battery. The gun he had wasn't found so that amounted to no evidence. Lucky muthafucka. My ego won't be able to stomach that. *Something* will be done. Sure will.

In the meantime, I decided to make it a point to acquire her all new and better shit. The punk ass nigga stole her white fox fur jacket, raccoon full-length fur, her mink and a full-length white leather white fox fur trimmed hooded coat. He jacked her DVD players, music, movies, digital cameras and camcorders. The jewelry she had was also taken from her at gunpoint. She had a Lady Rolex; a baguette iced necklace; a two-carat princess cut diamond ring; one-carat VS diamond earrings and a ten-carat platinum diamond bracelet.

All that shit he took from her he didn't spend a dime to get it. The nigga was leakin' and apparently jealous even though she laced his ass on the regular. Jane't was his bread, butter and seasoning. No wonder he snapped out. He never had shit. Not even a stack of the twentysix g' s he raped her for. A straight-up ass bum.

So I personally took a rode trip down to Chicago and spent nearly thirty thousand dollars on her. I went to Adriana's fur store on Michigan Avenue and bought her a hooded full-length chinchilla fur. Fuck a mink. Then I went to a jewelry store in the Water Tower and bought her a two-carat diamond pendant and a platinum ten-carat diamond tennis bracelet. I drove over to the shopping center in Oak Brook and bought her two DVD players and a two thousand dollar gift certificate she could use to get all new music and movies. At Sears, I bought her a new camcorder and digital camera.

All this new shit is just the start of all the shit I can do for her. I'm a man that knows how to polish a jewel like Jane't. If she'll let me, I'll make her a made woman.

When I got back to Milwaukee I called her up and told her come over to my place cause I wanted to show her some things.

She had absolutely no clue what she was going to see but when she does, the girl may faint and I'mma *have* to call the paramedics. One thing is for certain, women love expensive gifts. Makes them feel special. On the other hand, I'll go over to her place to see what's up with her.

"Say girl open the door, what the hell are you doin' in there?" I asked her.

"I was just drawing up my bath water cuz I really need to get in it and handle some business if you don't mind," she sassed.

"Oh that's cool. I wouldn't want you to be feeling not so fresh and your pussy smelling all tart. There's nothing worse than a smelly ass cat," I laughed.

"Look here boy, don't get on my bad side cuz I can cut you," she spat.

"Nah, I wouldn't want for you to slice me to shreds over nothing so just go on and take your bath and I'll watch some cable."

"Cool, make yourself at home and there's some juice and water for you to drink and fruit to munch on in the refrigerator if you want it. I won't be too long babe."

Perfect! While she's in the tub scrubbing clean for the king, I can sneak out and smuggle all her new shit in the house and lay it out for her.

A whole damn hour later, Jane't emerged smelling fruity and looking oiled down. She still hadn't walked into the living room so I had to call her in.

"Hey J, come on in here for a quick sec I want to show you something."

She hollered, "Ok, just let me get something on my feet right quick."

When she sauntered into the living room her mouth fell to the floor at the sight of the chinchilla coat. She swept the room with her eyes and took in all the other shit I bought her and the next thing I knew, she squealed like a pig getting slaughtered. The most deafening sounds came from her. It was worse than sitting in a classroom and hearing someone with Freddie Krueger nails scratching the chalkboard. Eerie. It baffled me when she began to cry.

"P, what did you go and do? I know you did this to make me feel better about what James had taken from me but you really shouldn't have. I can't lie, I miss my shit but I got my shit on my own, I didn't have it bought for me and I wouldn't feel right taking all of this beautiful stuff from you."

That revelation made me want her to have it even more. A true woman would reply like that. A simple ass gold digger would've taken that shit and ran with it doing a hundred miles per hour.

"I want you to have this stuff because I believe you didn't deserve to have your shit stolen from you. Baby, this stuff you see is nothing to me. I'm not just a boss player. I'm a honcho. Honchos do this type of shit and its nothin', so your just gonna have to accept it cuz I won't take all this shit back and that's that," I informed her. I had to stand on her neck.

She looked at me like I lost my fuckin' mind. I probably did breakin' bread like I did. But it ain't trickin' if you got it like that.

Lookin' Out

I need to catch up with my dog Loc and see how he was doing. I called him on his cell phone and we had set a time to meet up for lunch downtown. My guy was obviously stressed out and apprehensive about the indictment list that was coming out. The niggas in Milwaukee nowadays preferred to bitch up and snitch rather than handlin' their situations like thoroughbred soldiers.

According to Loc, a few cats had already opened their mouths about him. Like a true gangsta he badly wanted to x those marks and their closest family members as payback. I didn't like to talk about his future murderous plans cuz somewhere down the line I could possibly be sweated for even knowing about the conspiracy. I'm not a rat but I don't need the faggot ass pigs gruntin' around me either.

Other than that, he had a new first baby on the way and happy as hell about it. With the baby due in June, Loc still wanted his payback. He may get sent up for quite some time being a prior felon. He asked me to be the baby's godfather. I felt honored. Hell, I don't have any kids of my own but to be asked something important like that is honorary. Even to a thug like me. I'll most def look out for his shorty ' til he touches down again.

That's what friends are for. Some muthafuckas will stab you in the back and leave you for dead. True friends won't pick up the knife.

To ensure that his baby and its mother could sustain while he was gone, he entrusted me to the knowledge of a secret spot where he had close to a million dollars stashed. I had to look out and make sure his family had a nice home and some stability until he comes home. This stash wasn't in Milwaukee and no one else knew where it was. As long as I'm alive and well that stash is going to be right where it is.

For one reason or another, the feds must have been timing their attack. Just two weeks after his baby was born the marshals went to arrest Loc. I do know that ever since Jewel was born, Loc wouldn't leave his family for shit. He wouldn't even leave the house to holla at me. No amount of money, food, clothes, or just kickin' it could make him leave the house. In the event that anything was needed he sent someone to go for them. I felt like that nigga that worked for the governor on that tv sitcom back in the days. You could have just called me Benson.

Jewel was a lovely caramel baby girl with a head full of curly hair and she weighed in at seven pounds and eight ounces. It was too soon for me to really tell who the newborn lizard looking baby resembled more, but I've never seen Loc so close to tears. Hell, all newbies resemble lizards to me.

Personally, I believe the boys could have arrested him sooner but knowing that his baby was about to be born it seemed like they waited on purpose. At least he got to spend time and take pictures with his little girl because he was facing ten years to life if he was convicted on all the counts brought down on him. However, due to a prior gun conviction it really ain't no tellin' how long he may really be absent from the bricks.

My only responsibilities were to make sure mother and daughter were straight and that he was cool.

A few other cats in the hood were round up as cattle also, except for one named Tiny. He wasn't going out without a fight and when the boys went for him, he had a stand off with the muthafuckas. If Tiny was apprehended, he would have been facing the rest of his life in prison, a thought I knew he couldn't stand to bear. The stand off made the news and papers everywhere.

The boys in blue didn't know just how much heat Tiny had with him. He had AK-47s', a couple of Desert Eagles, hand grenades, and sniper rifles. The nigga was a real life walkin' tall one man army. Weapons he bought from some of his Mexican buddies on the Southside.

It was goin' down like Armageddon on the block before a barrage of bullets finally killed Tiny. He had took out three federal officers with the guns. When about twenty of them stormed the house, Tiny was already hiding up in the attic. He had a special spot from where he dropped the grenades down on them. It was the worst takedown in the city' s history. The total count dead including Tiny was twenty-four.

My guy took out twenty-three pigs before he left this world. I had to ask myself if I were facing life would I take anyone out with me? Might as well.

The Brief Lockdown

A few ladies were arrested as well. One in particular, known as Cherry was on the indictment list too. She would transport kilos of cocaine from California to Milwaukee by way of train, bus or plane. The girl was ruthless.

Cherry was holding so hard niggas would sweat the shit out of her because they knew she was a thoroughly bred hustla'. She was doing her thang for several years before her name was put out there. The woman was only twenty-nine with two kids, a 600 Benz, mini-mansion, platinum and titanium credit cards, jewelry, sable furs and whatever else any female could ever want.

Her dad was a well-respected dope dealer whom she learned the game from. Her brothers were too young in the head to handle the pharmaceutical business so her father handed her the reigns.

The dope game wasn't the only shit she knew though. She had two degrees from the technical college in Milwaukee. By looking at her, you wouldn't have been able to tell she was running the streets of Milwaukee by selling dope.

She was facing twenty years for her hand in the game. Money laundering and tax evasion was charged on her. Cherry had a few coin laundries and car washes that were legitimate, so it was tricky for the feds to confiscate all her properties and possessions. Her kids went to parochial schools and were spoiled. Their father was killed in a drug deal gone bad two years after they were born making her the sole provider and parent. Its not like being a single parent was hard for her because her dad had major chips.

Another guy who got caught up, Big Tev, was handling much of the dope Cherry brought in town plus he was the weed man. Tev was hustlin' ever since he was sixteen down off of Locust Street. He made a move that saved him some years in federal.

Last year, he made the decision to not move any more heavy dope, just the weed. Big Tev never had a rap sheet and if the government was only going on hearsay about his dealings, they would lose that case. And not only that, but Tev never would touch or deliver his own product. He had a myriad of younger studs doing the dirty work. That way if anything were ever to jump off by the time his formula was figured out, the weed would have already touched at least eight different hands. Therefore making a strong felony drug case against him was weak and futile.

Lastly, a Californian cat named Riko who was affiliated with the L.A. gangs was brought in on charges too. Since he had two strikes against him already, this last case would land him in prison for life. His connections hailed from the far west coast to all of the Midwest regions like Chicago, Detroit and Minnesota. When he first landed in Milwaukee no one knew him and that was a good thing. A year later, everyone who sold narcotics knew of him and his reputation.

With all of the major players being locked up, that left a handful of young hungry niggas in training on the streets to take over. These young whippersnappers liked to live life in the fast lane disregarding the notion that connectivity was the key to enjoying life after the game. The young cats liked the pussy, the jewelry, the cars, rims and clothes not caring that all of those things could have been stripped away from them. I ain't mad at them.

They had names like Young Dog, Bird, Yak, Lil Bubble, Ahmad, Black, Mac, Big L, Dough, Mu-Moo, Dyke and Taz. Some lived to have fun with their fast fortunes and some were set up, some even murdered by their so-called friends.

It's a battlefield in the hustle world. It's about survival of the illest, not the fittest.

I was able to avoid the major drama but hell, the boys in blue hauled my black ass in on suspicions of being part of the big conspiracy.

I don't know who in the hell spoke my name into some bullshit but I do know that once I got in the holding room I saw damn near all of the major players handcuffed and gettin' ill.

Everyone was just sittin' around looking at each other. The room was so silent a muthafucka could hear a roach crawl on the concrete floor. Heads were hanging low and every person was deep in there own thoughts.

"Who the fuck in here know the hell is going down?" That question came out the mouth of a young baller who went by the name Rims.

Some folks just looked up at him and shrugged their shoulders, but a female offered an explanation as to why everyone was in there.

Her voice was low and even as she mumbled, "I know for a fact that everyone up in this joint serves, so I think its only obvious that we all been indicted."

This bitch went by the fruity name of Peaches. She was five feet four inches tall, light skinned and she wore her hair in a short style. She was a known hustler off the East side of town.

"Aight little girl, you real smart heh?" Rims asked that question with sarcasm in his voice.

"Nigga, you the one who asked the dumb ass question in the first fuckin' place so don't catch no attitude up in here. Hell if I didn't answer your punk ass, you woulda asked the same dumb fucking question again."

As grim as it was in the brightly lit holding room undercover giggles could be heard.

"Yea, ok. You got jokes right now but you betta be glad I'm cuffed the fuck down right now or you' d be picking some of your teeth off the floor right now hoe," Rims shot back at her.

"You bitch ass nigga! If you ever think that you could get away with raising yo' hands my way you need to rethink that bullshit.

Now them other hoes you fuck wit' probably g' d for yo' garbage, but I don't know your small time nothin' ass. In fact, I'm tryin' to figure out why your sorry ass up in here anyway. You ain't heavyweight nigga."

Peaches pulled Rims hoe card and made him feel small on the inside. He knew that she was telling the truth. Rims got his name on the streets from jackin' other niggas cars and stealing the rims to only sell them to the highest bidder who wanted them. From that money he made off the rims he would then buy a couple of pounds of weed to smoke and sell.

"Awe beeyotch, you don't know what the fuck I do beyond what you think you know but when I get outta here, I'll be glad to show yo' ass with this here ten and half foot of mine."

"Fuck you and yo' foot boy! As a matter of fact, didn't you just steal the rims off a champagne Cadillac Escalade and sell them to that nigga Cash?"

Talk about puttin' the business out there.

Every single niggas head looked up at that point. Rims felt everyone's eyes on him and changed his demeanor a little bit.

"First of all, I ain't stole nobody' s rims, I stopped that shit a long time ago. You betta be glad yo' ass don't have any rims because I would bust down and take yo' shit. Don't be surprised if you wake up one morning and the hubcaps be missing off your raggedy ass Pinto, bitch!"

The room lightened up a tad bit with laughter. Even Peaches had to laugh at that crack.

Shit got back to seriousness when the door opened up and two detectives plus two uniformed pigs walked in.

One of the two detectives was none other than Brunette. He was looking like he just emerged from a corner snorting some white girl. The rim of his nostrils were red.

"It's good to see all of yall in here havin' a good ol' time at the taxpayers expense. Ain't it Willis?"

Willis was Brunette' s partner in crime. Willis had been on the police's drug unit force for less than two years.

He used to do shit by the books but once he saw how easy it was to take kickbacks from the players on the streets his integrity quickly faded. Why shouldn't it? What cop wouldn't want to take in an extra couple grand a week tax-free?

"I think they all in here having a little bit too much fun if you asked me. I know I wouldn't be laughing too much if I were handcuffed and sitting on cold concrete."

Brunette then spoke, "Look, we're sure you all don't want to be all night or for the next few days for that matter. I'm not gonna pussyfoot around with you people either. All of you are here because of an ongoing investigation. Each one of you will be interrogated individually. Depending on what comes of your questioning you'll either be released or held for further questioning."

Willis chimed in, "Pretty soon yall will be able to eat some cold cut sandwiches. Does anyone need to go to the bathroom, ' cuz if you do then you need to speak up now or forever hold your piss or shit."

Peaches raised her hand to go use the stainless steel toilet in the ladies rest room across the hall.

I raised my hand to signal I need to take a piss. My bladder was full from drinking all that day.

The two uniformed officers stepped over to handcuff each of us and escorted us out into the hall.

While I was taking the eightball piss I was trying to figure out who I could call that had a phone to accept the charges besides my mother. The last thing I wanted to do was bother her with my nonsense. Besides, the boys in blue had nothing on me anyway. I never sold any crank to them plus I strived to keep my shit on the low low. As of late the only thing they could try to fuck with me with is the pimpin'. The bright idea popped up in my head on who I could call …

Jane't.

Opening the door to leave out the bathroom a uniformed officer gestured for me to come his way. We ended up walking past the holding room to another room that looked more like an office with a desk two chairs and a computer.

The uniformed officer I was with spoke to me for the first time, "you can go inside and someone will be in here to talk to you in a minute.

"Can I use the phone?"

"Sorry. The phones aren't on and can't be used unless they're cut on from another room."

Damn, was all I could think to myself. I hope I won't need an attorney for this bullshit, because the only attorney I know for sure in the game that could get charges dropped at the drop of a dime taxed no less than twenty thousand to take a serious case. Her reputation in the city was impeccable being that she only dealt with the folks that she knew could pay her her worth.

Old school big time dope dealers chose to deal with her back in the day. A lot of cats were facing life sentences with over thirty counts over their heads, yet after fucking with this attorney they ended up only dealing with fifteen or less counts.

Attorney Stacey Worthington was her name. Her track record was exceptional. She went to Spelman college in Atlanta, Georgia and graduated magna cum laude. Then she relocated to Milwaukee to attend Marquette Law School. Upon graduation, she worked for the top criminal law firm in Wisconsin for two years before deciding to branch out on her own.

Her case record involved criminal cases of all sorts. With a winning track record of three hundred forty-two wins to seventy-six losses her reputation and status as a competent attorney was well known and appreciated. Ms. Worthington had even been featured in the Wisconsin's top one hundred lawyer magazine. She respectively was in the top fifteen percent.

She's a bad bitch.

If they try and charge me with some bullshit, I'm just gonna have to cough up the dough and retain her because I don't care to spend a day in jail for no damn body.

Snitches will shake so much salt in the game to make themselves look as if they really didn't take part in any wrongdoing.

Loc's name has been shitted on so tough no amount wiping may be able to help him. Being that I was his right hand man regardless of the fact that I didn't actually deal drugs could be enough to put me under. I ain't going out like that.

Luckily for me, the boys really had nothing substantial to keep me on so I was released four long ass hours later.

I went on to the house and layed up deep in my thoughts.

Grown Man Realizations

All this time I thought I was a man doing manly things like buying houses, pimping, selling, delivering dope, fuckin' a lot of nothing ass broads and making a name for myself in these streets but I was wrong. I was still a boy ...

For one, even though I handled my biz I was still playing. I was focused more on money than my small family. But whatever I did was for the cause, the family. I may appear to be a grown ass man but my philosophy is that I'm still a babyboy until I can't go to my mother anymore. I hope I did all I could to show my mother how much I love her. I hope I somehow eased the load she was carrying. I hope I wasn't a burden she couldn't handle or get rid of. My goodness, what roads am I going to have to face when she leaves me in this cold ass dump of a world.

I never knew my father like a son should have known his dad. If his punk ass were ' round to help my mother life would have been easier on her, on us. If his ass ever cared about my momma he wouldn't have left her to raise me alone.

If his ass was a real man he would have married her and made us a family. If his punk ass were a true man, my momma wouldn't have had to turn tricks to make ends meet. If his ass were a true man, my momma wouldn't have had to steal to put clothes on our naked backs and shoes on our bare feet. If he were a true man, maybe I wouldn't have had to be in the streets trying to make mom's life just a bit easier even though she got it going on.

I never knew my grandmother or grandfather, aunts or uncles, cousins, brothers and sisters. El was dead, the only nigga I considered my brother and he's dead. When my only relative I know leaves me, I'll be alone in this cruel ass world. My dogs are all getting locked up. I don't have a steady woman in my life, no one to love and call my own. All shit I need to fix.

I don't have any children, shit my mother hasn't had a grandbaby to see, touch and feel. She may never get the chance to change a grandchild's pamper. Sometimes I wonder, am I a failure? I need someone to talk to who'll understand my emotions. I need some real companionship. Like LL, I need love. I should holla at Jane't. She's wife material.

Arriving on the block, I noticed that the lights were on at her house and her truck was parked in the front, so maybe I'll be lucky. Hopefully she isn't busy or anything.

She came to the door looking like an around the way gal and she invited me to sit on her navy blue leather couch. Relaxing on her sofa I vented my frustrations to her and she listened without interruption.

After I finished exposing my feelings, I felt like a straight up bitch. She came closer to me kissing me lightly on the lips while hugging me for what seemed like forever. The shit happened just like that scene from *Boyz In The Hood*. She smelled like peaches and her body felt supersoft. I ain't gone lie, I want to hold her forever if I can.

Before long, we were necking and making love with our clothes on. I never did that before with anyone. Normally it was all about the suckin' and stickin' but making love doesn't always have to involve sex. After we took a much-needed nap, she told me about some of her issues and it was my turn to listen.

A Lil' History

I can't believe all of the gorgeous things P bought me. He must really think a lot of me to spend the type of money he spent.

Jane't was deep in her thoughts while she looked at all the new stuff in her possession. She hadn't ever encountered a man who went all out like P did. Any and every thing she ever owned she had to get it on her own.

I met James at a strip club on a winter night a couple of years ago. I was bored at home and decided to check up on one of my hoes at the strip club on the other side of town.

My life back then was as gravy for a female as it could possibly get. I mean I paid dirt for rent in the sum of twenty-five dollars. My utility bills were included in the rent. So every single month I only had to come out the pocket a total of damn near seventy-five dollars to cover my living expenses. The other fifty went on the home phone.

I know your probably wondering how the hell was I able to get by like that just like everyone else wonders. The game is normally sold but since you bought this book it has been sold right? Well dig the lick ...

Before I left home, I always knew that I didn't want to pay high ass rent somewhere. I set out on a mission to find some affordable reliable housing.

So I got in the Sunday newspaper and looked under the rental sections for low-income housing. I came up on this ad for an apartment complex that had openings for new tenants. I then called the number associated with the ad.

The lady who answered the phone advised me to come in and fill out an application before the end of the working day. I went to spot, picked up the application and filled it out in its entirety.

Upon handing the application back to the woman she told me that I should hear something within the week but before I left out the door, she browsed the application and saw that I was in college at the university. That must have scored points with her because she addressed the information she saw. I told her what year I was in school and what I was studying. It wasn't hard to tell that she was impressed. From the surroundings, I could see that she would be impressed with me from the type of folks she was used to dealing with on the daily.

What I mean by that is this, bear with me. I wasn't the only female in the office filling out applications for housing. The other broads I peeped in the building didn't appear to have their heads screwed on too tight. Perhaps it was a lack of education. Perhaps it was poverty. However, once hearing a couple of them speak I quickly came to the conclusion that they just didn't have the upbringing that I had. It doesn't take a rocket scientist to figure out that a couple of them never finished high school and if they did, they just barely made it.

Hearing how the other broads spoke made me cringe inwardly. It's not difficult to tell the difference between proper English and that dysfunctional term for broken English that's only applied toward black folks called ebonics. Now let me explain why I cringed inwardly. I felt embarrassed because I peeped how the lady who was accepting the applications looked at the broads. She had that look on her face that said-"Here comes another dumb nigger."

Well I was mad and sad at the same fucking time. I was mad as hell at the fact that here was this white bitch looking down on my fellow sista. Hell, to tell the truth I don't really know what ethnicity the heifer was, she could've been Polish, Russian, Australian or whatever the fuck. All I know is that she had a slight accent and she was non-ethnic. This bitch was snobby yall.

I was sad as hell because I wanted to know who in the fuck were these broads parents who didn't care to keep their feet implanted far enough in their daughters asses deep enough to make them sit their dumb asses in school long enough to learn something besides the dumb ass questions that came out of their mouths.

I know it ain't just me that hate it when it's that lone, one black person that sets the whole nation back one step due to ignorance. Yall know what the fuck I'm talkin' about. If your reading this book then I know you've probably watched the news at some point in your life and when a news reporter was chronicling some breaking news type shit in the hood, the only person the reporter always seemed to pick to interview was the horrible speaking muthafucka who just looked like they couldn't spell the word interview correctly even if a measly hundred bucks was on the line. Don't play dumb you know what I'm talking about.

Anyhow, I had to give the accented speaking hoe a smile as I left because regardless of who was all there filling out applications, I was determined to be the first person accepted into the apartment complex. My impression on the buzzard was solidified.

One whole week went by, and I hadn't heard anything from the apartment complex so I got on top of my game and sweated them. I called and left inquiry messages as to the status of my application on a Monday. Come to find out the broad that was accepting the applications was actually the apartment manager who made the decisions as to who comes and who goes.

Well, my impression impressed her to the point where she remembered exactly who I was. She told me to come in for an interview and to bring my social security card, driver' s license or state identification, tax returns or school grant and loan information with me. The interview was set up for that upcoming Thursday afternoon.

Hell, I figured if she wanted me to bring that much info with me that I was sure to be one of the applicants that was getting an apartment.

That Thursday rolled around and my appointment had been set for one o' clock. I had my black ass there at twelve fifteen postmeridian. I wasn't playing any games with this shit. I wanted my own apartment and I didn't want to pay a lot for it either.

I was definitely there super early because ol' girl was out to lunch and wouldn't be back until a quarter to. Whenever I make appointments anywhere I already know to bring something with me to keep me occupied so I brought Ice Berg Slim's book *Doomfox* with me. I didn't care what time the manager came back in after her lunch because the book kept me happily and content until it was time for me to handle my business.

She finally came in at ten to one. She noticed me as she entered the office. The buzzard was all smiles. Don't fade me, I was all smiles too. I was damn near willing to put on some blackface makeup if needed be to accomplish what I set out to do ya' dig.

She was again impressed with my thoroughness and appreciated my capabilities in having all the necessary paperwork she asked

me to bring in a neat folder. I went through the normal questions and she asked me if I had any children or a boyfriend that would be in the apartment with me. I had neither and that seemed to ease her mind. All she could rightfully assume was that I was just a lucky black high school graduate that was a second semester freshman college student and all I wanted and needed was an affordable apartment to live in while I studied.

When she saw the name of my high school on the application her interest in me was even more peaked. I'm sure she recognized that my high school was parochial. I definitely wasn't the average.

Anyhow to make a long story a little bit shorter, I got the apartment and was given a move in date that was approximately two weeks from whatever day that interview was on. The only thing I had to come back to her with to pick up the keys were the security deposit and first month's rent. No problem.

The security deposit was only two hundred and fifty dollars and the first month's rent was two hundred and forty-one dollars. The rate of my rent was calculated according to what I made on my job.

At the time I was working at the largest bank downtown. I had had that job for several months before my apartment hunt took place.

She was so gleeful in giving me the apartment she asked me if I was interested in looking at the apartment that day just to make sure I wanted it. Of course I accepted the offer I wanted to see exactly what the fuck I was getting myself into.

The apartment complex I would be living in was located not to far from the east side of Milwaukee on a busy street. We arrived at the building. The building was three stories high with a black- gated fence surrounding its perimeter.

I couldn't help but to think that it was like Fort Knox but it was cool with me. I can adapt to any situation.

We walked up three flights of stairs to the third level and my apartment number was twelve. There were twelve units in each building. She put the key in the door and I was like whoa. The place was pretty neat for the neighborhood I was in.

The living room was large and the windows gave me a top flight view of the streets. The bedroom was a pretty nice size too. I could easily fit my queen size bed in it with plenty of room for the dresser and chest.

The bathroom was decently sized as well. I wouldn't have had to worry about being crunched in like some bathrooms are made. Now the kitchen was different. On one side, the refrigerator, stove, sink and cabinets and the window in the kitchen faced the busy street. The apartment had a total of three closets. Even though I was a little disappointed that there wasn't any carpeting, I figured I could have some carpeting installed if I really wanted to.

The place was freshly painted and clean as fuck. I was ecstatic. My very first apartment was going to be lovely. I was even happier with the notion that unlike some of my buddies who moved away from home, I didn't have to have a roommate. I know I didn't want a roommate anyway. I'm too private for that.

When we got back to the offices, I told her that I would bring the monies she needed the following Monday. I was informed I would get the keys at that time and I could start preparing the place even though my move in date was slated for two weeks away.

I got in my short booty Buick Riviera and started to mentally lay out my new place with decorations. Long beforehand I had been preparing myself for getting my own place so I had saved up nearly a thousand dollars. Coupled with the financial aid I was getting for that semester, I had close to three thousand to spend as I pleased.

Being prepared for shit was my forte. I didn't like going into shit half-assed. I had my checkbook with me, so I decided to go to Target to pick out some bathroom and kitchen shit.

When I got to Target, one of my favorite stores, I grabbed a shopping cart and went immediately to the bathroom section. I picked out a navy and light blue bathroom set up that included a waste basket, toilet and bath rug, toilet seat covers, two shower curtains, toothbrush and soap holders and plenty of bath and hand towels. I had at least two hundred worth of shit just for the bathroom alone.

My decoration skills are impeccable. I already knew that once I got finished decorating that bathroom it would look like a shit palace fit for a queen. It definitely was going to be cozy and plushed out.

The two most important rooms in any home ought to be the bathroom and kitchen. I walked over to the kitchen section and picked out a four-sliced toaster, a blender and a box of pots and pans all made by T-Fal of course. I also picked out some kitchen curtains and rods. I wasn't going to be the type to hang sheets and shit from my windows. That was bullshit. I guess you could say I was too bourgeois for that garbage. The last shit on my list was cleaning supplies. So I had to step to that aisle and get my garbage can for the kitchen, scented trash bags, mop, broom, bleach, ammonia, Ajax, scouring pads and bunch of other shit.

By the time I made it to check out I had two full carts of merchandise with me. My total damage for the two hour shopping spree at the store was close to three hundred dollars. Not bad at all.

My next immediate plan was to drop all that shit off back at home and then go out to Sears warehouse to shop for some furniture and tvs.

I made it out to Sears two hours before closing and came up on a thirty-two inch television on sale for a couple of hundred dollars. The furniture department was off the hook. I found a navy blue leather couch with a thirteen hundred dollar tag on it. Now dig this, I had heard about people coming in to this store and changing tags on shit. Yall should know that a college student can't afford to spend that much money on furniture. So I did what I had to do and I switched the tag on it to have the price of only two hundred and sixty dollars on it. I borrowed that tag from a leather couch that was damaged.

I had to really make the shit look legitimate by calling over one of the sales associates working the floor and I played my part of being the consumer seeing a price on an item and expecting to get it for exactly that price.

I don't know what it was but the floor person didn't appear to give a damn about the tag being low as hell on a couch that didn't have any visible damage. What I didn't know was that both sides of the couch was supposed to recline but only one side was able to. So that helped me out.

I went to the counter with the sales floor associate with the tags in hand for the television and the couch and he rang me up to a total of five hundred and some change. A bitch was happy yall to be able to pull that move. I had set up the delivery for an afternoon drop off.

All I had left to do was to pick out some carpets for the floors and get a microwave and I would be set for the basics. For the rest of the stuff I needed I figure I'd only spend five hundred more and use a thousand of what I had left to prepay my rent in advance five months. I was pretty damn good with money for an eighteen year old.

I went on home satisfied for a day's work on my day off from work and school. All I needed to do was secure phone service for my new apartment and I could take of that from home. Yea, I stay on top of my shit.

After I officially moved into my new crib, the months were good to me. I was able to deck my pad out even more. Walking in my shit a person would probably think that I was rich or my parents straight looked out for me. My parents looked out for me enough. I wasn't twenty-one but I was grown. I had to handle grown ass situations.

I ended up getting fired from my job at the bank for being lazy. Hell, I was developing carpal tunnel from punching in numbers on the machine so damn fast. I only got lazy after it was my time to punch out. The supervisor in the department where I worked didn't want to let us all punch out until the work was complete for this one account. This bitch wanted just a little too much from the kid so my half-slick ass tossed the remaining checks in the garbage.

Well what I didn't do was look around hard enough to see if anyone was watching me. Apparently, some one was and told the boss what I had done. The goofy looking broad went to the exact garbage can I threw the remainder of the accounts in took the bag of checks out and waltzed over to me with them. She ordered me to key in the checks and let everyone else clock out.

I felt sooo incredibly fucking stupid I wanted to crawl underneath the keying machine and hide. I ended up staying after hours a whole half an hour because of my laziness. My dumb ass.

When I went into work the very next day I had plans to speak with my supervisor and apologize but she had other plans for me first.

No sooner than I sat down to start up the machine I was called into the office. I knew something was up but didn't quite exactly know what. Anyhow, I went into the office and was asked to close the door.

The supervisor pulled out my work history file and commented on my tardiness to work a couple of times. Then she commented on my inability to follow the rules. It didn't take too long for her to tell me that simply because of my insubordination the previous evening that I was being relieved of my duties. She informed me that I was getting a two week severance pay and that I was going to be escorted from the building and wouldn't be allowed back in for any reason.

Now look here, I don't know if she thought I was gonna break down and cry or what but I was tired of the damn place anyway. I took my firing like a champ and quietly gathered my few belongings and left with the escort. I had never been fired from a job before but I ain't gonna lie, it didn't feel all that damn good. I felt like a reject. I truly believe though, that from that experience I thought that perhaps working for someone else wouldn't be my thing for life.

Ok, I clued yall in on that to bring you to this point. Being that I was living in low-income housing, any change in income had to be reported.

When I got home that day, I had called the office and informed them that I was no longer working. Procedure was that when a resident was no longer working the rent would drop down to zero for only that month. Oh, I could hang with that all year if they let me. But the next month, it was raised to twenty-five bucks. The government handled the rent payments. Cool.

So here I was, a college sophomore at this particular time, paying only twenty-five dollars in rent. I was having my way. I lived off of twenty-five dollars rent for nearly five years.

Getting My Twerk On

In my third year of living at the apartments, another government program had openings for what's called rent assistance. I definitely was interested in that so I went and filled out an application for that too. The waiting list was for a couple of years and my number would eventually come up.

I had no problems waiting for that time to come around because I was doing just fine right where I was.

It was in my four and half year stint at the apartments when I met James.

Now since I wasn't working I had to make some type of income in order to maintain.

On certain nights of every week I kicked it at this one particular club. Because of my connections to entertainment icons, I was favorably viewed as a very important person. My entrance into this club was never denied and no matter how long the line was outside, I didn't have to wait to get in where I fit in.

Well, at this club called Tap One, I was hanging with the gangstas, the drug dealers, the hustlas, the strippers and the prostitutes. For some reason or another I just felt comfortable as hell around all of them.

Visualize a college girl in the company of whom I just described above. Yea, I still went to the frat and sorority parties.

In fact, I was even on line for a sorority. But I did what the hell I wanted to.

One night a strange gal came up to me in the bathroom and asked me if I danced. I don't know where the hell she got the nerve to do that but I way say that whenever I did step in the place, like Tupac, all eyes were on me. I think folks knew that I was a tad bit different from them when it came to lifestyles. I'm sure they had clues to what I was doing scholastically because I occasionally sported my signature college gear.

Anyway, I told the broad who asked me if I danced. Nope. And I was in college. She gave me the compliment that I had the body to shake my ass. I was intrigued because I had seen many dancers get their groove on at the club. Those girls would make their asses jiggle and the men seemed to enjoy it a great deal. Whenever I got on the dance floor it also seemed like they expected me to make mine do some hydraulic shit. Believe me, I knew how to do it because I would get my dance on in the privacy of my apartment but I didn't care to do it at the club for everyone else' s pure enjoyment. Fuck all that.

The bathroom broad wrote her number down on a piece of paper, handed it to me and told me to call her if I were ever interested in giving dancing a chance. Oh I was interested alright, 'cause those hoes would come to the club wearing beautiful furs and big ass rocks on their fingers that later on I eventually viewed as being cheap ass cluster diamond rings.

I ended up calling the girl later that week and chatted on the phone for all of half an hour. Within that time she had informed me that the amounts of money I could make in one week would be more than what I would make working a decent paying job. I was g' d for that. She invited me to go on a trip to Indiana for a week. Jacked up thing was that to go on this trip to Indiana I would need drive because she didn't nor did she have a car.

Ok, now I was a bit confused by that revelation because the numbers she had spit my way about the game made me believe that any woman who was making the amounts of money she quoted my way oughta have a reliable nice vehicle.

Oh well, we finalized the plans for this trip for the following week. It was on me to get some dance outfits and shoes. I went to the mall and stopped in Frederick's of Hollywood. Keep in mind that I was green to this shit, so don't drop the book when you read what I bought.

I picked up a couple of outfits that I thought would be pretty neat to strip out of. The three outfits consisted of an army fatigue, a zebra patterned and lastly, a Wonder Woman ensemble. That's right, I was going to be the female Marvel comic strip superhero. My plan was to turn circles on that stage and a bright light was gonna flash at just the right time. I also picked out a couple of babydoll dresses off the clearance rack. In all, I bought like six outfits.

Old girl had given me the location of a dance store to go to get my shoes that was located down on the East side called Mr. Shoes. I went in there and marveled at all of the different styles of shoes he carried but I damn near fell out at the price tag on them. All of the damn shoes I looked at were no less than seventy-five dollars a pair and some were more than a hundred dollars. My face was screwed up so tough that the owner of the store immediately offered me a twenty-five percent discount if I was a dancer. I picked out two pair of heels, clear and black. Hell I figured those two colors damn near went with anything I had.

I had to dip into my savings to cover those expenses but I also came to the conclusion that if all went well I would recoup that and then some.

The day of the weeklong trip came up quick and I was actually looking forward to it. At that time there were two main black strip joints in Indianapolis. One was the decent club and the other was the straight up hoe club. Money was my objective and I was geeked off the thought of just making more than two hundred a day dancing.

Some girls would be shy and scared to get up on stage to bare their assets but my attitude was like I didn't roll all the way down here for nothing.

The club itself was ok I suppose. It was dark and mysterious with banging ass music. The dressing room definitely could have used some work but overall it was ok I guess. The bitches there were all up in my video and I suppose they could smell my fresh meat. I pull out my little costumes fit for Halloween, got undressed, wiped my pussy and ass with baby wipes, oiled down and put on my superhero outfit. I then went to pick out my music, two rap songs and waited my turn to get up on stage. The niggas in the club were looking at me like what the fuck. The other dancers were straight trippin' off of me too. All I knew that I was gonna get on stage and do that magic turn and that mysterious light was gonna flash behind me.

Walking around in the six-inch heels weren't difficult at all for me because I modeled as a kid. That was a piece of cake.

I peeped the chick that was on stage that I would go up after and that hoe could dance her ass off. I thought to myself that with some time I would be cold like that too.

The dj announced the little name I picked out for myself. I called myself "Foxy" that time around. The dj made reference to my human super powers and played started the music. As I walked toward the stairs of the stage I quickly peeped the crowd and prayed to the gods that I would get tipped something for my first time efforts. After my two song set I left the stage with about twenty dollars. I don't know if people were tipping me to encourage me or they tipped me because I was new or tipped me because they felt sorry for me but nonetheless, I got off that damn stage with twenty dollars. Throughout the night I noticed that some girls were lucky to make it off the stage with ten bucks so I didn't feel too damn bad.

The men did genuinely appear to like the shape of my body and like I told you earlier in the book, I was shaped up like Serena Williams minus the titties of course. I had ass for days with thighs to match.

I went back downstairs to the dressing room to cool down and freshen up and boy-o-boy those girls down there were busy chatting up a storm about who was doing who and who was doing what afterwards. A few of them commended me on my first performance and gave me some advice. Those girls were cool. I decided to change into one of the short tight lingerie outfits and went back upstairs. As soon as I got up there this dude pulled on me to come dance for him at the table. He tipped me five bucks and asked me to go upstairs to VIP to dance for him. The dances up there were fifteen dollars of which ten I got to keep for myself. He let me dance for him for four songs. Those were the longest four songs of my life but when I left from upstairs I was forty dollars richer.

Before long I was going up and down those stairs throughout the whole night. I even got the opportunity to eat with one guy who had ordered some food from the kitchen. A bitch worked up an appetite ya' understand.

A couple of hours before closing I decided to tally up my earnings and I had earned just over two hundred. Not bad for my first day I thought.

Now the broad that I came down with had made less than that come to find out. She asked me matter of factly would I have a problem with selling some pussy. Please imagine the look on my face when she asked me that. Sell pussy? For how much? How long? Where? Those were the questions I needed answers too.

She put me on that I should demand no less than a hundred. A hundred dollars just to fuck? Geez, I fucked for free back at home if I liked a nigga like that so to get a bill for the pussy seemed quite appealing.

Not to put yall totally in my business but I'll put it to you like this: for the three days I was down there I made twelve hundred dollars from dancing and whoring. I never counted that much money that fast from my legitimate job. It would have taken me two months to get that type of money after taxes.

My thoughts of working a regular job after that were null and void. When we got back to Milwaukee I immediately dropped ol' girl off and went to deposit my bread in my bank account.

I noticed how ol' girl was trying to count my pockets. I guessed that was normal. I never did like people all up in my smitty like that. I don't care if all I had on me was a buck fifty, it was none of your business.

I wanted to go back to Indianapolis that next weekend. I went and made just about the same amount of money. I estimated that I would have to pull at least four tricks out of the three day work week. No problem.

The best trip I went on up there was during the football classics. Everywhere was poppin'. I had a lot of fun. The club was more packed than ever and niggas were droppin' that bank the best way they knew how …quick.

In order to work at the club though, those of us who were planning to work had to be there for the entire week. Monday thru Wednesday was sooo slow. I was lucky to make enough money to cover motel and gas expenses. But for that entire week I came home with more than two thousand dollars. I was on a roll. All I needed to do then was stack my chips.

At least that's what I wanted to do.

Hustlin' Other Aves

Once I got back home from that last trip I wanted to take a brief break from working. I knew I had a good amount of money on cash reserve at the house. I didn't put those earnings in my bank account because I didn't want the apartment people to catch wind of how much I had to work with or they would've probably raised my rent or something. Didn't need that to happen.

During my self-imposed vacation, I shopped and laid my little apartment out.

I bought some African artwork for my walls and I started to order some raw ass pieces from the Pottery Barn catalog.

I went to JcPenny and bought some expensive eight hundred dollar carpets. Thing is, I didn't pay eight hundred for each of the three carpets. See, in the street game, you come into contact with all sorts of people. I met professional boosters who were ready, willing and able to get what I wanted. I met up with a few out there at the store and showed them what I wanted. Those girls put some clearance tags on those three carpets and I paid the store a total of just a little less than a hundred dollars for the carpets and I paid the girl who switched the tags for me three hundred. That came out to a hundred thirty-five bucks per carpet. I saved over two thousand dollars fuckin' in her business. I still have those hand-woven wool Persian carpets too.

Before long, I outgrew my apartment. I had so much shit in it that I needed a much larger space.

During my hiatus from working I came into contact with a couple of girls who wanted to get down. By this time I was a hustler in my own right. I was following the career of this Hollywood Madam in the news. This white bitch was getting rich off of her hoes. She ran an escort service that catered to real money spenders.

One night I visited this adult bookstore and picked up an adult newspaper. I bought a dance book that had every strip club listed in the United States, Canada, Japan and whole lot of other countries for about twenty bones. When I got home I looked thru the newspaper and peeped the advertising ads for the escort businesses. The ads contained the rates per half hour and whole hour that patrons would be charged for services. I was inspired to start my own shit up.

I'm not a dumb bitch so I did my research on what I needed to do to get my own shit up and running. It certainly wasn't hard. I decided to put my rates at one hundred seventy-five dollars for a half an hour and two hundred fifty dollars for a whole hour. I offered everything from full body massages to fetishes to dominatrix shit. I had a few girls that wanted to be on my team too.

I had to get another pager for business purposes and a second cell phone. The first couple of meetings I did on my own and my best day was seven hundred dollars for two hours total worth of work. Dancing at the clubs immediately went to the bottom of my list of how to get paid.

The girls that wanted to be on my team worked at a local strip club on the other side of town. I knew they would be cool with escorting for my business and paying me a lovely percentage of the profits.

Flossin'

One night I decided to go up to the club where my part-time employees worked at. I got dressed like the young gifted and black businesswoman I was.

I had put on this three hundred dollar jumpsuit I paid vittles for from the boosters and some high heeled leather pumps. I wore my full-length white leather hooded coat that was trimmed with white fox fur. The store I got that from was Fox' s men' s wear and that damn coat had cost me seventeen hundred dollars. I put my diamond studs in my ear and my ring on my finger. I was on point.

I left out the crib looking a feeling content with how my life was going. All my bills were paid far in advance. I had a nice stash put up in the crib. And I had put my beautiful Buick Riviera in storage and drove my new Cadillac Sedan DeVille. I was on top of my world. I was on point. And the best thing of all is, I was having my way by my damn self. I didn't need a man like some women starved for.

As I drove to the club, I listened to some EightBall and MJG. In fact, the song I played over and over again was On Top Of The World. I was chillin' yall.

When I pulled up in front of the club, I took inventory of the cars parked outside and noticed that a crowd was in attendance.

The Queen Bitch was about to step in the joint and the drones were gonna come my way too.

I got out my ride, chirped on the Viper alarm and sauntered gingerly towards the entrance. I was *all* woman. The doorman watched me as I was coming up and like a gentleman he was, he swung open the door for me a few yards before I reached the entrance opening.

Walking around the joint I found a table near the stage and was preparing to sit down when one of the club's security guards came over to help me out of my coat. Somehow without even trying to I commanded respect. My mere presence alone shook the spot. I liked the effect I possessed over people. It was smooth as silk. Plus it helped that I was a chocolate mousse cutie pie.

I took a seat and perused the crowd with my gaze. My eyes met up with this one stud a couple of times. I paid him no mind but eventually he got up the balls to step in my realm.

"Hello. Can I talk to you for a minute?"

Now here was a jerry curl wearing black ass fat muthafucka with gold in his mouth trying to holla. I'm sorry, lemme correct myself, he sported a wave nouveau and it was pretty too. If you notice I didn't mention his facial looks. He had big round pretty eyes, thick eyebrows and pretty shapely lips. He wasn't bad looking at all in the face.

I replied, "What would you like to talk about?"

I was all business besides, I already know the agenda on a nigga's mental.

We engaged in small talk and I kind of liked his approach so I gave him my number and instructed him to give me a call shortly. He did just that.

During our telephone session that lasted every bit of two hours I came to find out that he wasn't originally from Milwaukee. He was from another state down South. He had been living in Wisconsin for about a year. He had no children in Milwaukee and none cross-country. He finished high school didn't work a legitimate job and he shared an apartment with a relative of his.

I wanted to hear from him why he stepped to me in the club.

Yea, I wanted to know for my own ego' s sake. He mentioned that I was fine and looked interesting. Ok, I could deal with that revelation.

It was getting super late so I needed to end the conversation so I could shit, shower and go to sleep. Just in that order.

We made arrangements to hook up in the next few days to peep a movie and dinner.

He seemed like a cool dude nevertheless, I told him I would meet him at the restaurant. I didn't want to let him know where I laid my head at. For all I knew he could have been a crazed maniac and I didn't really want to have to put a cap in his ass.

The night came around for us to get together and I met him at a restaurant at the mall where the movie theater was also located. We had a nice time at dinner. The conversation was cool but I wanted some humor in my life. It seemed like he was trying awfully hard to be cool and collected.

I already know my piercing eyes penetrated the depths of his core. Yall must understand that I'm a cold ass bitch. I'm hot shit.

Testin' The Waters

A few weeks had gone past and James and I had become more cool with each other. We went out on more dates. We talked on the phone at least three times a day. All was cool.

I eventually felt comfortable enough around him to come over to my place to chill. When he finally entered my apartment for the very first time, he eyes went buck. I peeped him as he surveyed my living arrangements. I know he was in awe. Have you ever seen a shabby looking house from the outside but when you stepped in you were shocked to witness how nice it was on the inside? Well that's what he went thru because my apartment building was in the heart of the hood where it was all good with me.

We would order in food, watch tv, play board games and dominoes. We weren't officially a couple but it sure seemed like we were.

Over time, James earned a place in my bosom. I can't lie, it was fun having a male around who didn't mind doing manly things for me like taking out my garbage, and washing my whip. It was also fun to kick it to the movies every week.

I never let on to how I was maintaining my lavish lifestyle. The money was still flowing in. There were even times when I had to postpone our getting together to handle some monetarily beneficial functions. A hustler never stops getting at that cheddar no matter what. I certainly wouldn't stop because James definitely wasn't putting anything in my pockets.

Since I knew that he didn't work a job it didn't take much addition to come up with the formula that he sold drugs to fund his lifestyle.

I had been to his apartment was quite shocked myself that he and his relative actually held down a spot that looked like a home. Most guys I knew didn't have a fully furnished home but these boys did. That was major points in my book.

James may have been a big guy but he was neat and didn't harbor an offensive odor on his person. His breath on the other hand needed to be refreshed every now and then.

Guys with those gold and silver teeth don't understand that they get bad breath from those caps. A person' s tooth rots underneath that shit. Every so often I had to remind him to go brush his grill and gargle or to pop a mint in his mouth. He couldn't use those minor mints to freshen his shit. He had to dip into the major leagues of mouth refreshers.

It was a long six months before I let him tap my ass. My pussy was strictly for profit purposes only.

The night I did give him the booty he nutted within the usual two minute gap. I couldn't believe it. His dick was seriously minor too but I overlooked that because he was such a cool dude. I never really ever kissed his ass because his breath was strangely tart. When we tried for round two, the round where the guy was supposed to show what he was really made of, he nutted again but this time around he lasted about a whole minute longer.

I know I got some fiya ass pussy but damn, was this all I had to look forward too?

As our relationship progressed, I made him take me to the adult store to gather up some dildos that he could use on me. If I was going to continue this union he was going to have to use toys on me. That two and sometimes three minute shit was bound to make me go absolutely crazy.

It seemed like he and I were always in contact with one another and around each other too, so it hit me in the gut when I found out from a strange phone call in my presence that something just wasn't quite on the level.

Some broad had called his phone and he tried to play it off like the call itself was just about dope business. He apparently forgot that I wasn't a dumb girl.

My woman's intuition instinctively told me that there was more to that phone call than what he claimed it to be.

By this time it had been damn near a year that we had been fucking with each other. Now I was cool with a lot of shit but lying to me in face I was not. James had liar plastered all over his forehead in bright neon lights.

I asked him to call his "business" call back and he offered me opposition. That was it right there. I ordered him to hand me his phone and he complied like the good boy he was supposed to be. I called the number back and the girl must have thought that it was James on the line because she was trying to sound all sexy and shit. I identified myself and made the inquiry as to who she was and her purpose in James life. Her name was Lisa.

Lisa and I talked on the phone briefly for about five minutes. She had informed me that she had know James for about a year and that he had just left her place earlier that night giving her some money. I asked was their relationship based on business or more than just that. It came to my attention that their relationship was about more than just business.

Ok. I am not going to be a trooper about my so-called man giving some other buzzard money when he should have been dropping that bread with me. I'm the one who whipped up meals for his fat ass whenever he was hungry and even when he wasn't. I'm the one who laced his ass with gear he didn't even have the inclination to sport. I'm the one who had put up with his little dicked ass for the sake of feelings. Yet this fool still had the nerve to lose his rabbit assed mind by fooling around on me? Yea ok.

I ordered his ass to leave my spot in a low, even, calm voice.

As he was going down the stairway, I politely busted his head open with my bat. A blood trail could be seen going down the stairway.

I even hollered for him to wait outside until I came down because I wasn't done with him just yet. The mark knew I had a lead missle charger in the midst. I went to my panty drawer pulled it out from it's resting place and proceeded to go down the stairs to get up with his no good lying ass in the parking lot.

By that time his bitch ass hopped in his ride. He peeped what I was holding at my side while I was walking toward him and he stormed off hitting zero to sixty in four seconds. I'm surprised his engine didn't blow up from the sudden burst of speed. That nigga knew I was about to apply some serious pressure to his fat ass and he hauled court.

That night began the demise of the relationship we had. I couldn't trust him no matter how he attempted to apologize and beg. I was wholeheartedly faithful to what we had. For informational purposes, I wasn't even getting money in my business personally. I had enough girls online to do it for me.

A couple of weeks had passed and I decided to ease up on the cold heartedness. I thought that anyone who got caught fucking up should at least get the opportunity to prove themselves.

I know he tried yall. But I couldn't get it outta my head plus upon reviewing his cell phone records, I saw that he had indeed still been in contact with Lisa. But I never said anything about it.

Now this is where the tripped out part comes into play.

I made the decision to leave his ass alone period. All the shit I had given him he could have. That meant nothing to a giant like myself. I didn't need or want anything from him, so he was actually getting the better part of the stick on all that bullshit.

I think he knew that eventually I was going to be thru with his triflin' ass. I stopped allowing him to come by my crib. He no longer got a hot, delicious meal cooked from within my pots and pans. He certainly didn't gain any access to the ass. It was a snowball effect.

Now during the last few months I had been in contact with precious and he had been by my house.

One day P was leaving my pad and my phone had started to ring. I didn't think shit of it so I answered it. It was James on the other end. He wanted to come thru to talk to me about something urgent he claimed.

Little did I know that he had been sitting outside my house already casing out my joint. I told him he could come thru for just a minute. That was a mistake because the activities that took place after that nearly cost me my life.

What happened in the end of that whole ordeal showed me a totally deranged other side of James.

I was pistol-whipped, beat and robbed.

I had to go to the hospital to get twelve stitches in my ear from where I was hit with the butt of the revolver. James held that revolver to my forehead. He held that revolver to the back of my head after he flipped me over. He even held that revolver to the crack of my ass.

My life flashed before my eyes. I believe when James saw the thick blood oozing from head that sight jerked him awake from the crazed state of mind he was in. I won't ever forget that he said he would kill himself after killing me.

November thirtieth is a date I won't ever forget yet it's also a date I must not ever forget to celebrate.

That revolver did not have a safety switch on it. That revolver was fully loaded too. The graces that be prevented me from being another statistic of the crime of passion.

I hadn't ever broken it all down to P. But he knows now. They say when someone does dirt to you to let God handle it.

There's no plan better than His I hear. Yet I have a plan too. Just when I'm going to execute it is the question that needs to be answered.

TO BE CONTINUED

Same GRIP Time
Same GRIP Handle

ACKNOWLEDGMENTS

I've opted to shorten this section considerably. In the original version it was quite lengthy.

My fans: Thank you for supporting my book amongst the many others to choose from. I truly love accepting your phone calls to me. Hearing your praises and congrats mean an awfully lot to me and don' t even worry, the sequels to, Don' t Knock The Hustle, will be available to you shortly. With each work, I'm continually growing and nurturing this literary craft. I am re-entering this game with my head screwed on more tight than before. I'm on MY mission this time around my friends. I lost contact with thousands of you on social media due to my page having been deleted. I hope to reconnect with all of you soon.

To the celebrities who had reached out to me about MY SHIT!! I don't know any other author who has had rappers on deck with them like me off the rip.

Chad "Pimp C" Butler- you called me on several occasions and gave me yourIZM about my endeavors. You have no idea how much I miss recieving your calls. You are dead and gone and I hope you know the rest of us still here still RIDE DIRTY yo! I don't give a fuck what ANYone claims, you didn't die..you were murdered! I am so sorry that I didn't come to Texas when you told me to. I still regret that to this day mayne. I miss you Pimp. #UGK for life!

Michael "Mystikal" Tyler- Oh my fucking gosh! When you called me several times weekly..meant so much to lil ol' me. My mommy would get to rapping your cut DICK ON THE TRACK, lol. Thank you so much for reaching out to me and loving me. I'm fucked up because yo' weak ass people won't put me in contact with you. I am going to thoroughly sweat that bullshit soon yo!

David "Styles P" Styles- SMDH....WOW! I did not even have a clue that you had tweeted about me on Twitter! Thank you so much for that. I'm going to be calling you soon yo! In fact, when I make my way back to New York, I plan to ride down on you and Jada.

Terence "Drama" Cook- Yo my ninja! Thank you for contacting me. I need to find you.

Ezekiel "Freekey Zekey" Giles- Thank you so much for reaching out to me. To have had a Diplomat holla at me was like whoa yo! When I come back to the East, I cannot wait to hook up with you one time!

Demetrius Flenory "Big Meech"- To hear from you was like OMG! Keep your head up yo! You are a celebrity too!

A beautiful soul and given me encouragement and his advice entering the literary game and I shole would love to be able to speak to him these days. Mr. E. Lynn Harris...your encouragement and blessings for and to me meant alot to me. I enjoyed our conversations immensely. I only hate that I did not get the opportunity to meet you in person before you left this wicked earth. Thank you.

I must give a shout out to my damn self! I paid for this with my own GRIP the first time around and will always do it. I was fortunate enough to not have needed to write my script and hope someone else would publish me. I put myself on. There's a lot to be said for that alone. Quite a few authors from my era had to go the other route and got played. But that's not my battle. My gangsta flex is STILL strong!

Most importantly, I give all my thanks and blessings to my Higher Spirit for granting me the strength when I felt I wasn't strong enough; for granting me the wisdom when I wasn' t knowledgeable enough; the vision for what I needed to see even when it was blurred. And certainly for keeping me safe from those who only wanted to cause me harm physically, financially, emotionally, and mentally. More importantly, my Higher Spirit for keeping me from harming them. #HOTEP

LIFE IS SOMETHING ELSE! Open your THIRD EYES yall!

INSIGHTFUL QUESTIONS FOR AUTHOR

Q. Your cover art is different for this title. Why didn't you or your publisher opt to use models for the cover book's design?

STACY: The non-use of models for this title was truly intentional. I had a vision for Don't Knock The Hustle and that vision did not include wanting it to resemble the countless other urban fictions on the market. Besides, the title itself carries more than enough weight. Hell, the currency is the model.

Q. Were your intentions to make Precious the protagonist or an antagonist?

STACY: I intended for Precious to inhibit characteristics of both. His entire life revolved around hustling. I needed Precious to have conscious thoughts and conversations with himself on certain situations that you the reader should see.

Q. Different characters all had their unique way of hustling to get by. Please expound.

STACY: Living life is a hustle. Those whose mentalities are narrow would only assume that hustling involves illegal activities. Here is a short list of hustlers: Slave owners; Presidents; Colleges; Prisons; Judges; Wall Street Brokers; Republicans; Democrats and Banks. Hustling isn't limited to drug selling, prostitution, gambling and misappropriation.

Q. How close are you to the characters you created?

STACY: Certain characters in the book have a resemblance to me. Some characters are amalgamations of individuals that I have come into contact with at one point or another.

Q. It seems as if you glorify hustling. Why?

STACY: No matter what it is you do in life, it's a hustle, an artform within itself. Hustling to attain and accomplish a goal can be beneficial, no matter what that goal is. The con is, it can also be detrimental.

Q. Where is the sequel?

STACY: The sequels are in development. Each work will show growth. Yet, I will not write fairytailish novels. I have other genres in the works as well. I do not wish to limit myself.

Q. You' re an author who is accessible. Why?

STACY: I have read other books and wanted to get the opportunity to interact with an author and never could. I wanted to make sure that my readers would get the opportunity to communicate with me. These days other authors have followed suit and now make themselves available to their readers. I did it way back in 2004 though.

Q. Some say the streets do the choosing. Do you feel the streets chose you?

STACY: I chose the streets. I come from a well to do upbringing. I chose to play in the streets. I hang in the hoods by choice. Some of thee most authentic and philosophical people I know are the crack heads, drug dealers, prostitutes, robbers and thieves. Why bother sugarcoating shit? The real will come out in the end. Some folk had to be in the streets for no options were available. I have and had options, yet and still I chose to get on the grind. I respect the grind. I could go on an on til the break of dawn on this, but there's no need.

Q. Any closing words for your readers?

STACY: I thank each and every one of my readers for purchasing my book. I know factually that I have let many of my fans down with not staying in this publishing game. I thank each and every one of my readers for contacting me. We all have our own struggles to deal with. It gets greater later. The hustle is what the hustle does. I'm back on my mission yo!

ORDER FORM

SN HOLDINGS LLC
PO BOX 742164
DALLAS, TEXAS 75374

Don' t Knock The Hustle

$14.95 Include $3.95 Shipping/Handling for one book and $1.95 for each additional book (Via U.S. Mail) Canadian orders must include payment in US funds, with 7% GST added.

PURCHASER INFORMATION

Name _____

Organization _____

Reg. # (Applies if incarcerated) _____

Address _____

City/State/Zip _____ Phone _____

Email _____

Total Number Of Books: _____

Payment must accompany orders. Allow sufficient time for delivery. Accepted forms of payment: Money orders, Cashier's Check, Institutional Checks, Postage Stamps. For personal check please allow 7-10 business days for clearance from your banking institution before shipment. Please allow 4-6 weeks for delivery.

STACY NELSON is the author of **Don't Knock The Hustle** and is a radio personality in the Midwest. She has appeared in television commercials, modeled in calendars and fashion shows, plus, performed as an exotic entertainer. She's acted in a motion picture as well.

Stacy Nelson currently resides in Dallas, Texas, yet, has not made a decision on her final resting destination. She is very active on social media, welcomes fan mail and brief phone calls.

She's in the struggle and striving, believe that.

www.ingramcontent.com/pod-product-compliance
Lightning Source LLC
Chambersburg PA
CBHW071005280626
47160CB00016B/2730